THE PELICAN FABLES

THE PELICAN FABLES

A Novel

Ian Grey

iUniverse, Inc.
New York Lincoln Shanghai

THE PELICAN FABLES

Copyright © 2006 by Ian Grey

iUniverse books may be ordered through booksellers or by contacting:

iUniverse
2021 Pine Lake Road, Suite 100
Lincoln, NE 68512
www.iuniverse.com
1-800-Authors (1-800-288-4677)

This is a work of fiction. All of the characters, names, incidents, organizations and dialogue in this novel are either the products of the author's imagination or are used fictitiously.

ISBN-13: 978-0-595-37435-9 (pbk)
ISBN-13: 978-0-595-82277-5 (cloth)
ISBN-13: 978-0-595-81828-0 (ebk)
ISBN-10: 0-595-37435-2 (pbk)
ISBN-10: 0-595-82277-0 (cloth)
ISBN-10: 0-595-81828-5 (ebk)

Printed in the United States of America

For Chad

CHAPTER 1

▼

MELBOURNE

Carter trembled as he continued up the long, landscaped drive leading up to the Monroe Building, which housed the administrative offices as well as several dormitories, the main dining hall, the mail room, the bookstore, and the Rappahannock Grill. It was a world different from any he had ever known—a world where he was to teach young men from some of the most prominent and powerful families in the country. Carter wondered what he, a poor kid from Mississippi, could possibly teach the children of senators, CEOs, CFOs, ambassadors, and trust-funded mothers and fathers that they did not already know. By the age of fourteen, when most students entered the Melbourne Preparatory School for Boys, the students had probably seen and experienced more of the world than Carter had ever even hoped to see.

He meandered through the long, wooded drive through the forests of Melbourne before passing into the expansive clearing, where the manicured grounds of the main campus began. The Monroe Building came into view. It was much larger than he remembered from his interview. His eyes scaled the massive white columns of the classic Virginia portico that dominated its facade, which, he had been told more than once during his first visit to the school, had been designed by Thomas Jefferson.

There was an empty parking space in front of the building, between a black Rolls-Royce with Texas plates and a vintage Mercedes from the District of Columbia. Carter shifted the gear of his Volkswagen Rabbit into neutral and turned off the ignition, causing the engine to shudder before the tailpipe coughed out a blackish puff of smoke. Carter looked around self-consciously to see whether the disruption had been noticed and was relieved that no one appeared to be in sight. He took a deep breath and exhaled slowly. He looked in the rear-view mirror and brushed his golden brown hair with his fingers. He had just had his hair cut a few days before he left Mississippi. The barber had cut it a little too short, but Carter figured it was better to err on the short side, which would fit in better with the conservative environment of the school. He checked his teeth in the mirror too, and then rubbed the front row with his index finger to make sure they looked shiny and clean. Carter was more self-conscious about his appearance than someone with his good looks needed to be, but his self-awareness had more to do with his being somewhat shy and awkward than with any of his physical qualities. He had a lean, athletic build, deep brown eyes, and thin, long eye-lashes—features that made him almost as pretty as he was handsome.

Carter opened the door of the car and stepped out. A fashionably dressed woman in a fitted knit suit was descending the wide circular stairs leading from the entrance of the Monroe Building. At her side was a young boy who looked no older than twelve or thirteen. He was wearing a navy blazer, khaki pants, and a red and blue rep tie. Undoubtedly the boy was there for an interview. No one was accepted to the Melbourne School without having at least one interview for the fewer than one hundred or so openings for which the best, brightest, and most privileged boys were made to compete. It was all so foreign to Carter, who had not even owned a tie until he was nineteen. He began climbing the staircase.

"Hello," the woman said as Carter passed her and the boy on the stairs. Her accent was southern but sophisticated, like the high-cotton women from the plantations dotted across the Mississippi Delta.

"Hello," Carter replied sheepishly.

The woman gently poked the boy in the arm with her knuckle, which precipi-tated a "Hello, sir" from the young man, who was probably under intense pres-sure to make a good impression.

"Hello," Carter repeated as he passed the boy on the stairs and then walked through the tall, black doors of the Monroe Building.

"May I help you?" a shrill woman's voice called out as Carter stepped into the entrance hall.

"Oh, hello," Carter began, peering into the reception room to his right. "I'm Carter Moran. I'm the new English teacher."

"Oh, yes," the woman began excitedly. Her hair was pulled into a large, thick bun on the top of her head, and she was wearing a pastel-colored polyester suit.

She looked exactly like some of the Pentecostal women Carter remembered from Mississippi—reliable and sturdy, but with no frills, like an Impala station wagon. "We've been expecting you. Just go down the main hall there and take your first right. Go all the way down, and then turn right again when you can't go any further. Then go all the way down to the end. You'll think you're about to fall of the face of the Earth, but you'll get there. By the way, I'm Sophie Winchester, the switchboard operator. I was on vacation when you interviewed."

"Nice to meet you."

"Yes," Sophie Winchester continued. "Well, don't keep Mr. Wirth waiting. Run along."

Carter walked down the hall of the administrative wing, as he had been instructed. The walls were covered with black-and-white photographs of each of the successive entering classes of the Melbourne School, marked "Third Form 2004," "Third Form 2003," and so on. Unlike the Mississippi public school that Carter had attended, freshmen were not known as freshmen, but as members of the Third Form, or "Third Formers." Sophomores were known as Fourth Formers, then Fifth Formers, and finally Sixth Formers. It was just another indication to Carter of how different everything was at Melbourne.

Carter studied a few of the faces in the large composite photographs that were taken of the new students or "new boys" when they first arrived at the school. The returning students were not subject to this protocol. Rather, only the "new boys" had their pictures taken. The monumental images of each entering class were hung successively along the walls leading to the headmaster's office, only to be moved down one space each year to make room for the next entering class, thus marking the first right of passage from being a new boy to an upper classman. The boys in the photos looked so young to be so far away from home and bore little resemblance to the young men that Carter had met during his interview. But then it was Melbourne's credo to forge solid men out of the young, sometimes fragile boys who filed into the school year after year. Carter remembered passing through the photo-lined hallways during his interview almost a year earlier. Classes had just started, and Carter could not help but noticing that the photographs of certain students, mostly the scared or awkward looking ones but also a few who looked overly cocky, were heavily smeared with fingerprints, which signaled that these students would be the subject of intense hazing by upper classmen during their early days at Melbourne.

"Oh, hello, I'm Carter Moran," he said to the secretary at a desk in the waiting room outside the headmaster's office. The room had been the same during Carter's first visit to Melbourne for his interview. From the looks of the place, it had not been changed in several decades. Beige, low-pile carpet covered the floors from wall to wall, except for a few small Oriental rugs that were placed near the seating areas to add a touch of warmth or elegance to the room, which was otherwise somewhat austere.

"Yes, Mr. Moran, so nice to see you again. I'm Shasta Brockman, but I wouldn't expect you to remember that."

Carter wondered how anyone could ever forget meeting Shasta Brockman. With her snow-colored hair, leathery skin, and hot pink lipstick, wearing the same Kappa Kappa Gamma pin on her blouse that she'd had on the first time Carter had met her during his interview, she had made a memorable impression.

"No, of course I remember you. It will just take me a while to get all the names down," Carter replied.

"You'll know them all soon enough. We're a small community—tiny, really. You're not married, if I remember correctly, are you, Mr. Moran?"

"Uh, no, but I've just finished my master's program, so there's plenty of time for that, I guess," Carter replied, smiling awkwardly.

"Well, we'll have to see if we can do anything about that while you're here. There are lovely girls from some fine old Virginia families right here in Fauquier County who'd just love to meet a handsome young man like you. And maybe if we marry you off, we'll get to keep you here. I know that's what Mr. Wirth is hoping for. Now wouldn't that be nice."

"Well, I'm, uh," Carter began as sweat beads exploded across the back of his neck. He had assumed the question of sexuality might come up at some point, but had not expected it to come up so early or so directly. He had only recently begun to feel comfortable with the idea of being gay. With his classic good looks, he had repeatedly thwarted the advances of girls with whom he had gone to school. At least at Melbourne, he had hoped this would not be a problem.

"Oh, I didn't mean to embarrass you. Look at you, only here a few minutes, and I have you walking down the aisle. Just ignore me. But, of course, if you're interested, I'm a member of the DAR, the UDC, and just about every other civic organization worth belonging to, and I know all the prettiest girls from all the best families."

"Well, I'm only here for a year—"

"Oh, there I go again," Shasta Brockman interrupted. "Let me tell Mr. Wirth that you are here." She paused and then spoke into the intercom on her desk. "Mr. Wirth, Mr. Moran is here to see you," she said, smiling coyly. "Please have a seat, Mr. Moran. He'll be right with you."

Carter sat down in a nearby wing chair covered in gold and blue flame-stitch fabric that was beginning to wear through on the armrests. He looked around the room to avoid having to make further conversation with Shasta Brockman.

A huge clock was hanging on the wall across from him, and he watched as the minute hand slowly swept across the dial, each second seeming longer than the one before it. A few black-and-white photos in silver frames on an antique side table showed Mr. Wirth shaking hands with people who were probably important, but whom Carter did not recognize. He examined the antique gold curtains that hung from the tops of the tall windows to just an inch or so above the carpeted floors.

The room was as lifeless and timeless as the black-and-white photos on the table, preserved unchanging for future generations of students for whom the conservative décor would appear as constant and unwavering as the rigid standards the school sought to maintain. Carter thought about the opulent curtains he had seen while touring several of the plantation houses in Natchez, curtains that had puddled to the floor with no evident regard for the expense of the fabric or the time of the people who had to care for them. Such excess would never have been tolerated at Melbourne, which prided itself on its stoic principles and rigid moral standards.

Carter looked up as the door to the headmaster's office finally opened.

"Mr. Moran, Jake Sommerville, assistant headmaster. Come on in." A tall, heavyset man walked quickly to Carter's chair, his hand extended. He could easily have passed for a judge from any of the small towns littered across the rural South, with his well-worn seersucker suit, ever so slightly wrinkled, a thin film of sweat across his brow—like the kind of judge who carries a revolver behind the breast of his jacket.

Jumping from his seat, Carter shook the man's hand, which was thick and beefy, the hand of a disciplinarian—but discipline was the main function of an assistant headmaster. Carter stepped into the wood-paneled office of Alexander Wirth, the headmaster, who stood behind his antique mahogany partner's desk, placed precisely in the center of the room. In contrast to the staid atmosphere of the waiting room, the headmaster's office seemed somewhat warmer. The paneled walls were dark and rich and could easily have belonged in the interior of a prestigious gentlemen's club, with dark, rich curtains, a leather Chesterfield sofa, and Chippendale armchairs. Carter noticed a gilt-bronze inkwell resting neatly on the embossed leather surface of the desk. It looked like the kind of room where million-dollar deals were made, filled with cigar or pipe smoke and the slight cling-clang of ice floating in bourbon or scotch in heavy-crystal, old-fashioned glasses.

"Mr. Moran, so glad you're here," said Mr. Wirth. "I'm sure you're tired. Drove all the way up from Mississippi, did you?"

"Yes, sir," Carter replied, remembering the last time he had met with Alexander Wirth, whose demeanor was so formal and rigid that probably no one had ever called him Alex. With his perfectly tailored pinstripe suit and distinguished brow, Mr. Wirth looked more like a Wall Street banker than the headmaster of an all-boys prep school in the bucolic foothills of Virginia horse country.

"Please have a seat."

Carter sat down and crossed, then uncrossed, his legs.

"Don't be nervous, Mr. Moran. We're all family here. And I won't beat around the bush. I know we have you for only a year, but we'd like for you to consider coming back after your fellowship is completed. Now, that said, during the time you'll spend with us, we'd like to see what you can do—how you interact with, bond with, and lead the students. Anyway, this will be a challenging year for you, and we're glad to have you aboard."

"Thank you, sir. I'm grateful to be here," Carter replied, wondering how many times the headmaster had given that exact speech, but, more importantly, wondering whether he would even be sitting in the headmaster's office of the Melbourne School if they knew he was gay. This was only the third or fourth occasion that Carter had openly admitted to himself that he was gay, even if he still had no idea whether he would ever act upon it. But for the first time, sitting in the formal, almost repressive, atmosphere of the headmaster's office, he began to feel even more comfortable thinking of himself in this way. Perhaps it was simply knowing that his sexuality would have to be suppressed for at least another year that brought these relaxed feelings to the surface. *But*, Carter thought, *I've suppressed it this long, so what's another year?*

"That's fine, then," the headmaster continued, calling Carter back from his thoughts. "I know you probably want to get settled in. So, Mr. Sommerville here will show you to your quarters."

"Thanks again," Carter said as he stood up and shook the headmaster's hand.

"All right, then," Mr. Wirth concluded, signaling that the meeting was over.

*   *   *   *

"This is C Dorm," Jake Sommerville said as they walked toward the door to what would be Carter's apartment. The dormitories were the same as Carter had remembered from his interview, when he had been given a tour of the campus—far more Spartan than the public rooms of the Monroe Building. Like the other dormitories, each floor of C Dorm had its own sitting room with a small kitchenette, where students could watch television, make popcorn, or eat pizza they had ordered from town when their attendance was not required elsewhere. The floors were all covered in grey indoor/outdoor carpet, and the walls were stark white with dull brown trim.

Carter arrived with Jake Sommerville at the entrance to what would be his apartment; it had a paneled door that contrasted with the flat, painted doors on all the dormitory rooms. He had learned during the interview that the single faculty were assigned to be dorm masters in each of the dormitories across the campus. Dorm masters conducted daily room inspections, counseled the students, assisted in the event of an emergency, and monitored the general goings-on around the dorms. Most of the married faculty lived in well-appointed houses scattered across the fifteen-hundred-acre campus. The more elegant houses were occupied by more senior faculty, while the younger, newly married faculty lived in more modest but nonetheless attractive houses.

"It's not much," Jake Sommerville said as they stepped into the apartment, which looked as if it had not been painted or otherwise altered for at least thirty years. In contrast to the elegance of the headmaster's office, the apartment was more sparsely decorated with furniture that appeared as durable as it was ugly. The green and brown tweed upholstery of the sofa and chairs blended with the sculpted brown carpet, and the apartment had the odor of stale crackers, as if it had not been occupied for a while. But it was much larger than the efficiency Carter had lived in during college, and its furnishings seemed almost opulent in comparison.

"It has all the basics and should be very comfortable," Jake Sommerville continued. "You know, this was Bob Townsend's apartment. He's the professor you replaced. I think he even left some artwork. Yeah, see there," Jake said, pointing to a poster of the Metropolitan Ballet Company. "Kind of fruity, if you ask me. I always thought Townsend was light in the loafers. Something about him just gave me the creeps. You're not fruity, are you?"

"Uh," Carter responded, stupefied, wondering whether Jake could see that he was flustered by the question. His feet began to sweat.

"Oh, I'm just kidding. Of course you're not. We check into that kind of thing as best we can before we hire anyone. Wouldn't do to put some fruit around a bunch of pubescent young men. That's the problem the damn Catholics have, ya know."

"Yes, they've had their share of problems," Carter responded, beginning to regret having accepted a job at Melbourne. But his fellowship at Harvard would not start for another year, and this interim position would allow him to save a little money before moving up to Boston, which he knew would be expensive, despite the generosity of the stipend he would be given. Since Melbourne provided free room and board, Carter hoped to save most, if not all, of the twenty-nine thousand dollar salary he would earn during his nine months there.

"Anyway, C Dorm is a Third Form dormitory," the assistant headmaster continued. "You shouldn't have any problems. Mason Bird is the prefect assigned to this dorm. He's pretty straightlaced and should keep a tight lid on things. I don't expect you'll have any problems."

Carter had read in the Melbourne School's information packet that the twelve prefects were members of the Sixth Form who had demonstrated high academic performance, unreproached moral integrity, and superior leadership skills during their first three years at Melbourne. The term "prefect" derived from the Latin term *prafectus,* which means to place in front or put in charge. Becoming a prefect was the highest distinction that students could attain at Melbourne, and it guaranteed admission to any of the top colleges and universities in the country. The Prefect System, as it was known, was at the center of the Honor Code by which all Melbourne students were required to live. There were no locks on the dormitory rooms, no lying, no cheating, and no stealing. Students signed every examination with an Honor Pledge, a written promise that the Honor Code had not been violated. Even the smallest violations of the Honor Code would result in immediate expulsion from the school, but only after the violation was taken before the Prefect Board, which sat as judge and jury in determining whether a Code violation had taken place. Under the Honor Code's strict guidelines, a student could also be expelled for failing to report a violation by another student, even if the violation was only suspected.

"Anyway, if you have any problems or need anything," Jake continued, "just ask Mason. He and the other prefects will be here a few days before all the other students arrive next week. Mason is a nice kid, a little edgy, but a great guy. Of course, it doesn't hurt that his family has given over a million bucks to build the new student center here."

Jake Sommerville failed to notice that Carter had lost interest in what he was saying and continued in his monologue as if the new professor were all ears.

"But you know, some of these kids have a hard time living in the shadows of their parents. Our job is to pull them out, to help them be the best that they can be at whatever they end up doing. Anyway, enough of the soapbox. I'm sure you want to settle in. There's a faculty roster over there by the telephone. Don't hesitate to call if you need anything."

"Thanks, I appreciate that."

"Well, I'll leave you to it."

Carter closed the door and leaned back against it as he listened to Jake Sommerville walk away. Then Carter locked the door, thankful that, unlike the students, the faculty could lock their doors. He sat down on the ugly tweed sofa, which was firmer and more comfortable than he had imagined, and took a deep breath, unfastening his tie. The great expanse of the campus had not prepared him for how claustrophobic the school suddenly felt with its high standards and lofty expectations, standards that would never accept people like Carter—at least, if they knew the truth about him.

Over the years, Carter had perfected the facade that had protected him against all the hate, ridicule, and offhanded remarks directed at people like him from his adolescence until now. He had always been different from the other boys at the Copiah-Lincoln Middle School. He was smarter and more soft-spoken than other boys, and he held ambitions that stretched far beyond the lumber mills, slaughterhouses, and sharecropper farms that would later employ the majority of his classmates. And there was the unspeakable difference that Carter kept most hidden—that he was not attracted to women. It took several years before Carter could even begin to acknowledge, much less accept, the inescapable truth that he was attracted to men.

✳   ✳   ✳   ✳

Carter was seven years old when his father, Silas Moran, died. On that day, Silas said he was "fixin' to beat the tar out of Carter" because the boy had not wanted to go fishing, asking instead to stay home with his mother, Della, who was baking cookies. But then, it never took much to make Silas Moran turn violent, a fact evidenced by the frequent bruises, black eyes, busted lips, and other battle wounds worn by the lesser ranks of the Moran household. While these wounds might have attracted the attention of a teacher or a social worker in other parts of the country, the good people of Copiah and Lincoln Counties knew better than to meddle in other people's business, especially when the people in question were violent and unpredictable like Silas Moran.

Carter had been knocked to the floor of the kitchen when his mother walked in with a shotgun pointed at Carter's father.

On many other occasions, Della Moran had silently endured her husband's mental and physical abuse. Many times Carter had heard his mother whimpering in her bedroom several hours after Silas Moran had passed out either from too much liquor or from tiring himself out with the violence. There was no telling what had caused Della to do anything differently that day. Perhaps she had endured enough to no longer care about what the consequences might be from her sudden, unexpected course of action. Although Carter later speculated about what had caused his mother to snap, she and he never discussed what had happened. But then, actions do speak louder than words, and after Della Moran pulled the trigger, nothing more needed to be said. For whatever her reasons, she had finally had or seen enough to take an uncharacteristic stand.

"You wronged me, woman, and one day when y'ain't got your papa's gun, I'm gonna beat the ever-livin' tar out of ya. Hear me, woman? The ever-livin' tar. And when I finish with you, I'm gonna beat the ever-livin' tar outta that goddamn sissy brat too, gonna beat the goddamn sissy right out of him."

The last words Carter remembered from his father's mouth were: "Woman, you're the one that ruint him, turned him into a goddamn fairy. When a man's got to rely on a woman for protection, he ain't nothin' but a goddamn sissy-boy faggot." Silas had turned to Carter. "Sissy boy!" Silas heckled in a high-pitched falsetto. The words were more painful than the blows Carter had just endured, causing a wave of anguish to cut through his center, leaving behind deeper wounds from which he would never heal completely. Whenever Carter tried to come to terms with his identity, the old wounds ached from within him, causing the echo of his father's words "sissy-boy faggot" to reverberate through his entire body. It seemed that, while Carter had always known he was different from other boys, admitting this fact to himself was another matter. He found it easier to bury the entire subject deep within himself, sealed beneath scars that, at least on the surface, appeared to have healed.

On the day his father died, Carter had not cried, had not said a word. He just sat and watched life ooze from his father's body and into the weathered floorboards of the shack that was the only home Carter had ever known.

"Come on, son," his mother said softly after leaning the gun against the side of the kitchen cabinets. "I'll clean this up later. You gotta take a bath and get ready for bed." She pulled him up from the floor and into her arms as if nothing significant had happened. It took years for Carter to realize that his mother had probably been in as much shock as he was on the night she had finally put an end to Silas Moran.

Carter's eyes remained fixed on his father as his mother carried him from the kitchen and out of the room. Neither said a word as she brought Carter to the bathroom and watched him brush his teeth as the rusty cast iron tub filled with steamy-hot water. She placed a clean towel on the seat of the toilet and waited for the tub to fill. Then she closed the door and left Carter alone in the room.

He stood motionless as he listened to the coarse sound of dead weight being dragged across the kitchen floor and out the back door. Carter heard his mother filling a bucket and scrubbing the bloodstains from the old wooden floor. It was not until Carter could hear his mother rinsing the bucket that he remembered he was supposed to be bathing, so he took off his clothes and shivered as he stepped into the water, which had turned cool.

After Carter had bathed, his mother tucked him into bed without saying a word. The house was deadly silent, with only the faint sound of crickets in the distance. Then Carter broke the silence.

"Tell me about the pelicans, Momma," he asked softly.

"All right, son," she said wearily, sitting next to him on the bed. After a long, contemplative pause, she began:

This is the story of the pelican and the alligators. One day, the pelican was flying high in the air when a great big wind whooshed through the sky, knocking him right out of the sky. He fell to the ground with a loud thud and badly injured his wing so that he couldn't fly. A nearby alligator saw the pelican and thought he'd make a mighty fine dinner. He caught the pelican faster than a bolt of lightening. The pelican begged the alligator to spare his life, but the alligator refused, saying that chickens were his favorite food.

"I'm not a chicken," the pelican replied indignantly. "I'm a dragonfly, sent from the heavens to enchant the sacred waters of alligators, which are supposed to be the most magnificent creatures on Earth. But I must admit," the pelican said inquisitively, "I've never seen one of the majestic alligators. By any chance, have you?" the pelican inquired.

Then the alligator boasted proudly, "Well, in fact, I am an alligator."

"Oh my goodness!" the pelican exclaimed excitedly, and he bowed down to the alligator as gracefully as he could, but exaggerating the pain this caused to his injured wing. "This is the greatest moment of my life. I am so incredibly honored beyond belief just to be in your company, noble alligator, and I would be honored—most grateful, in fact—if you would eat me for your dinner."

Overcome by the pelican's flattery, the alligator set the pelican free. But not much later, after the pelican's wing had almost healed and he was once again soaring through the sky, another wind knocked him to the ground, where he was quickly captured by a different alligator. This alligator said he hated dragonflies because they were always landing on his eyes while he was trying to hunt.

"Why, I am not a dragonfly," said the pelican. "I am a pelican. And I eat dragonflies all day long. In fact, dragonflies are the only thing I eat!" And with this, the alligator set him free.

Carter's mother sat with him and rubbed his back until she could tell he had fallen asleep. She often told him stories at night; some she reinvented from tales she had been told as a child, and others she just made up. Carter had often wondered why his mother had even chosen the pelican as the champion for her stories. After all, pelicans were somewhat awkward birds, even gawky in appearance. But when they took flight and soared perfectly across the water—lowering their distended beaks into the waves, then raising their heads victoriously, nonchalantly—they had a splendid poetry about them. But then, it was Carter's nature to overanalyze. His mother was not a highly educated woman, although she loved books. She had been in her sophomore year of college when she met Carter's father, a handsome roustabout who worked offshore and who swept her off her feet. She became pregnant, quit school, and began the clichéd existence of a young girl who had made an unfortunate mistake and was too inexperienced to know how to fix it. But if falling in love and staying with Carter's father had been a mistake, giving birth to Carter had not been. She doted on him with single-minded purpose. Her attentiveness had given Carter the strength and confidence to achieve his goals, though lurking beneath the celebration of his accomplishments was a deep sadness and confusion. Despite his mother's obvious devotion to him, he feared that she might never be able to accept who he was. Though he wanted to please her, he was certain she would never understand homosexuality. Sometimes Carter resented his mother. After all, he thought, if it was acceptable for his mother to murder his father, why wasn't it acceptable for Carter to be gay? But Carter understood the thinking of the heavily Baptist, rural South, where situational ethics factored heavily into people's beliefs. After God had had enough of the likes of Silas Moran, he had given Carter's mother the strength and insight to put an end to him. Homosexuals, on the other hand, were an abomination excused by no extenuating circumstances.

On the night of his father's death, the police arrived and, familiar with Silas's violent nature, did not arrest Carter's mother, accepting her faltering explanation of self-defense. The county prosecutor did not press charges. Everyone in their small town, used to handling matters in their own way, knew that the world was better off without Silas Moran.

Not long after her husband's death, Carter's mother went to work as a clerk in a lumber mill. She often came home exhausted, sometimes teary-eyed, which made Carter wonder what kind of work could be so horrific as to turn the beautiful woman he saw into the sullen, downtrodden creature she slowly became. But no matter how tired and fatigued she was, being in her son's presence always made her seem more at ease, and he never tired of hearing her stories about the marvelous pelican that traveled the entire world.

Carter and his mother never spoke of his father or of what Carter's father had said the night he died. Carter wondered whether his mother accepted who he was or whether the subject was too painful or shameful for her to discuss. As despicable as his father had been, there was no doubt that Carter's mother had loved the man—but not enough to let him beat her or Carter even one more time. Whenever Carter thought about telling his mother that he was gay, he found himself unable to cross this boundary. After all, the shooting of his father had taught Carter that love has certain limits. Carter was unwilling to risk his loving relationship with his mother. More than anything else, he did not want to hurt her. She had already been through so much. Some things were better left unsaid.

CHAPTER 2

▼

ENGLISH TURN

Adam Proffit woke to the familiar sound of his father's Hummer H-2 pulling out of the driveway. "I knew it," he whispered to himself. "He always does this."

He rolled over in bed, more irritated than disappointed, but tried not to care one way or the other. This day had been planned for weeks. He and his father were supposed to play eighteen holes at English Turn, the gated community on the West Bank of New Orleans, where the Proffits had moved several years earlier. Adam had never played much golf, and all summer his father had been promising to teach him. But with only a week left before Adam returned to Virginia to begin his last year at Melbourne, apparently the promise was not going to be kept.

Fuck it, Adam thought. *I don't give a damn about playing golf, anyway.* He lay in bed for a while longer, trying to fall back to sleep, but the bright Louisiana sun was creeping through the louvers of the plantation shutters that covered his bedroom windows, making it difficult for him to nod back off. He finally crawled out of bed, shaved, brushed his teeth, and hopped into the shower. As the water splashed against his skin, he started looking forward to getting back to Melbourne and spending time with his roommate, Kellum Thurman, who lived in South Carolina and whom Adam had not seen all summer.

Throwing on a polo shirt and a wrinkled pair of shorts, Adam stumbled down the circular staircase that dominated the two-story entrance to the house. Adam remembered when the Proffits had moved to English Turn from Kenner, Louisiana, a lower-middle-class suburb on the outskirts of the city. Adam had thought the Proffits' house in English Turn was the grandest thing he had ever seen. But after spending three years at Melbourne, where he had been exposed to the way that far more affluent people lived, he began noticing that the house he had once considered a castle was not as grand as he had once thought, despite its having all the high-end accoutrements typical of houses in English Turn.

"Good morning, Adam. How did you sleep?" queried Elizabeth Proffit, Adam's stepmother.

"Fine, thanks. How about you?"

Elizabeth Proffit had been married to Adam's father for five years. While she had always been pleasant to Adam, and sometimes even tried to show a genuine interest in him, Adam knew that sending him away to Melbourne had been her idea rather than his father's. But regardless of who had made the decision, Adam was grateful for the opportunity to be away from home. He hated having to compete with Elizabeth for his father's attention and had decided even before going to Melbourne that he would not be a third wheel. But today was supposed to be different, because playing golf had been his father's idea—or at least, that's what he had been told. Adam realized that Elizabeth might have put his father up to it.

"Honey," Elizabeth began, "I'm so sorry to tell you, but your father was called away. One of the regional managers up in Shreveport is having a problem, and your father won't be back until tomorrow morning. He's so disappointed. You just don't know how much he was looking forward to today."

"Yeah, me too," Adam replied, resisting the urge to say something ugly. After all, she was just trying to be nice.

"Well, how about you and I go shopping for some school clothes? There's a big sale going on at Saks, and we can go to Brooks Brothers too."

"Oh, that's OK. I really don't need anything. But thanks, I really appreciate it."

"Well, you know, if you ever do need anything, you just call me. Your dad is always so busy, and it's easy for him to overlook that kind of thing. Here," she continued, rummaging through her Prada handbag and then pulling four hundred-dollar bills from her wallet. "Take this, just in case you need it or in case you find something you want."

"No, I can't take your money. Thanks, though."

"Honey, take it. It's yours too. Your daddy's the one who makes it. Take it, honey, please. I know it doesn't make up for anything, but it can't hurt to take it, either," Elizabeth Proffit said as she snapped her purse shut and placed it on the floor.

"I know you don't believe it, but your dad loves you. He's building all of this for you. Just for you. Now, I know sometimes that doesn't seem like much compared to spending time together, but it's his way to show he cares."

"I know," Adam replied. "Just, sometimes…" Adam began before stopping himself mid-sentence.

"Oh, honey. I know how disappointed you are. It breaks my heart for you. It really does," Elizabeth said. She buttered a piece of toast, brushing the crumbs onto her plate. "I was so close to my daddy. We used to go fishing, went to the Angola rodeo, camping—all kinds of stuff. Of course, that was when my daddy wasn't working offshore or drunk, which is how he spent the other two-thirds of his time. Gosh, during the depression, my parents grew up in a one-room shack down in Houma, and most of the time they ate bread and sugar water and were lucky when they had that much." Elizabeth giggled and drank more of her coffee.

"We barely had a pot to pee in, Adam, but I cherish those memories with my daddy more than anything in this great big fancy house we live in. So I can imagine how you feel. Anyway, I'm rambling like a crazy woman, but my point is that, as disappointed as I know you are, just try to remind yourself that he's really doing all this for you. I'm good company—you know, window dressing—but your daddy is doing all this for you."

"I know. Thanks, Elizabeth."

While Adam knew Elizabeth was trying to make him feel better, her words had the opposite effect because they only underscored that some of it wasn't true. Walt Proffit's sole motivation was making money. He lived for it. Adam had very little to do with it other than the fact that whatever he later inherited would determine how well Walt Proffit had done for himself. But then, all the hullabaloo about Adam's inheritance was likely to be just as shallow a promise as the one to spend the day together playing golf. If the deer-hunting, sport-fishing, man's-man Walt Proffit knew everything there was to know about his son, it was unlikely he would want to leave him anything.

CHAPTER 3

▼

AND THEIR EYES MET

As Jake Sommerville had indicated, the prefects arrived at school ahead of the other students. Jake walked beside Carter into the enormous main dining hall, which stretched all the way from the front to the back of the Monroe Building and into both wings. Massive wooden beams soared across the ceilings, giving the hall the atmosphere of an old hunting lodge. The floors were covered in red plaid carpet, and mahogany wainscoting shone from the bottom portion of the walls. Carter spotted a group of students sitting at one of the massive dining tables. *These must be the prefects I've heard so much about*, Carter thought as he followed Jake Sommerville to the table.

"This is Mason Bird." Jake began the introductions as each of the young men stood up and firmly shook Carter's hand.

They each said, "Pleased to meet you, sir" or "Welcome to Melbourne."

"Thank you," Carter repeated as he made his way around the table.

Carter had been uncertain what to expect of the prefects, about whom he had heard so much. They came across as confident, but not cocky, and determined, but not cutthroat. Some were more handsome than others, but they looked clean-cut and athletic, intelligent and respectful—possessing the attributes of excellence in sports, academics, and leadership. No doubt any one of them could become a U.S. president if that's what he set his mind on doing. These were the best of the young men that Melbourne forged from the cadre of students who probably arrived at the school with more polish and worldliness than Carter ever thought possible, especially because Carter was only four or five years older than most of them. While Carter tried to think of something to say, he felt intimidated by the prefects who exuded self-assurance without arrogance. He sensed that they were not simply the products of privilege, but also the sons of parents who had raised them to be humble, conscientious, and thoughtful—attributes that were honed and perfected at Melbourne.

*   *   *   *

The arrival of the remaining students presented a great spectacle. The formerly empty parking lot in front of the Monroe Building was packed with chauffeur-driven cars, taxis, and parents' cars, all dropping off students, some for the first time. It was easy to spot the new students riding in vehicles loaded from top to bottom with all the things they were thought to need during the next four years at Melbourne. Some boys looked teary eyed. Others appeared befuddled and weary, as if they were arriving for their first day at camp.

The prefects and other Sixth Form students were helping direct the parents of the arriving Third Formers, guiding them to the proper dormitories where other Sixth, Fifth, and Fourth Formers helped unload their cars and get the "new boys," as they were called, settled into their lives at Melbourne. Some of the new-student good-byes were very dramatic, with tears, wailing, and pleas to return home. Others were nonchalant, more collected, shaking their fathers' hands and kissing their mothers on the cheek, very formal and matter-of-fact. It was all part of the rites of passage into becoming a Melbourne boy. Just as easy to spot as the new boys were the returning students, who had an air of relaxed confidence—the same as the prefects, only in somewhat varying and lesser degrees. The returning students had no cars to unload, because they had stored all of their things in various rooms dedicated to this purpose during the summer.

Upon their arrival, all students were expected to purchase their books from the student commissary and check their assignments on the adjacent bulletin board. Carter wondered how the students could be expected to unpack, settle into their rooms, and still have enough time to complete their homework between lunch and dinner and before lights-out at ten PM, when everyone was required to be in bed. But then, he realized, these were the kinds of expectations thrust upon the young leaders who would emerge from the Melbourne School.

*   *   *   *

Carter sat in his classroom and checked his watch for the third time during the past several minutes. He looked down at his syllabus and then at the empty classroom of the Hanes Building to which he had been assigned. While built in the 1930s, the Hanes Building imitated the elegant Virginia architecture that predominated across the campus. In this way, Melbourne was not unlike a small version of the University of Virginia, with its rows of handsome Greek Revival buildings, well-manicured grounds, and ancient brick sidewalks. Carter studied the sixteen empty desks lined up in four rows and thought about the overcrowded classrooms of the Copiah-Lincoln public schools he had attended. In contrast to the forty or more students crammed into the antiquated 1970s classrooms of Copiah-Lincoln High, the average class size at Melbourne was about twelve.

Carter looked up as the students finally poured into class and took their seats. They were more casually dressed than Carter had expected, but Melbourne considered itself a country school and did not require uniforms, but instead had an informal dress code.

Melbourne students had a distinctive look, kind of preppy, but not like the fashion-conscious children of the doctors and lawyers of rural Mississippi. Instead of well-fitted, logo-emblazoned shirts and shorts, Melbourne students wore slightly baggy Bermuda-length shorts that hung loose at their hips. Their wrinkled oxford-cloth shirts had no logos and were tucked in just enough to remain in compliance with the dress code, suggesting a casual disregard for the expense of what they were wearing.

Carter sat down on the top of his desk and took a deep breath before looking up at the eleven students in English 601. They were quietly seated, waiting for Carter to initiate a dialogue. The class was different from public school, where the students were generally rowdy until the teacher instructed the class, "Settle down, people"—the universal public school signal that the lessons had begun.

"Hello, I'm Carter…Professor Moran."

"Good morning, sir," the students mumbled.

"As you may know, I've never taught high school before. All of my teaching experience was with undergraduates during my master's program. But based upon the accelerated academics here, I suspect this should not be too different. Anyway, please bear with me. I'm going to pass around a seating chart, with which I understand you are all familiar. Please fill it out."

Every class at Melbourne had assigned seating, another means of passive control to maintain order and decorum.

"The curriculum I've prepared for this semester is largely based upon the competing literary themes of classicism and romanticism," Carter continued. "The first two books on the syllabus are Jane Austin's *Pride and Prejudice* and Emily Brontë's *Wuthering Heights*. Within the next few weeks, you'll know these novels very well. Let's start with your first assignment. Who can tell me about the dramatic tension in the first few chapters of Ms. Austin's book?" Carter paused, waiting for a response. "As there are no volunteers," Carter said, examining the seating chart that had been passed around the room and handed back to him. "How about Adam, Adam Proffit? What can you tell me about the beginning chapters of *Pride and Prejudice*?"

Carter took a direct look for the first time at the student whose name he had randomly chosen from the seating chart. Adam Proffit was tall, about Carter's height, but with a leaner, more muscular build and short, sandy brown hair, parted unevenly to the side.

"Well," Adam Proffit began, "the Bennets are from an upper-middle-class family. Mrs. Bennet has several daughters and is totally preoccupied with marrying them off well. But this is made difficult by the family's limited financial resources. Then her daughter Elizabeth, the smartest in the group, wants no part in her mother's machinations to marry her and her sisters off. This will likely undermine her mother's plans and will provide dramatic tension from which the story will evolve."

Carter listened intently to the eloquence with which Adam Proffit effortlessly delivered his recitation about the beginning of the novel. Carter looked into Adam's eyes as the boy spoke and was slightly rattled to find the young man staring back at him, intently and intelligently. Carter had never felt such an electric connection with anyone, ever. It had been the subject of so many novels he had read—the sheer force of physical attraction between two people with a strong, immediate affinity for each other, so strong that others around them could sometimes sense it. Carter could almost feel himself being pulled toward Adam, if not completely into him, as though he were one of two magnetic poles being drawn to the other by the quantum physics of attraction.

Carter's entire body tingled from the electric static between them until he roused himself from his thoughts at the possibility that other students in the room could see or sense the sexual vortex between himself and this student. *This student*, Carter thought. He looked briskly away from Adam Proffit and out the window to break the connection between them. His sudden change caused several students to look out the window to see what had caught the young professor's attention.

"Professor?" Adam Proffit asked, redirecting his attention from the window. "Would you like me to continue?"

"Of course. I'm sorry. Just thought I saw something outside. Please, go on."

As Adam continued to speak, Carter felt himself drawn back into the maelstrom of the boy's stare, which made all the other students invisible to him.

Then the worst thing that could have happened began to happen. Carter could feel himself becoming aroused. At the same moment, Adam pulled at the crotch of his Bermuda shorts to adjust himself the way that jocks sometimes do, and Carter could not help wondering whether Adam was experiencing the same attractive force. Carter hung on every word the boy spoke but wished Adam would finish so that he would not have to look at him. Carter's body became moist with nervous sweat, sensing that everyone in the room had noticed the bulge that was forming inside his khaki pants.

"Thank you, Mr. Proffit," Carter said anxiously when Adam had finally finished speaking. "That was brilliant. OK, now, someone else. Let's see, Mr. Weathersby, why don't you tell us about the dramatic elements of Ms. Brontë's novel."

Weathersby began, and although this student was also well-spoken, Carter was relieved not to feel any peculiar connection with him. Carter did not call on Adam Proffit for the remainder of the class and avoided making any further eye contact whatsoever with him. When the class finally ended, the students stuffed their books into their backpacks and filed out of the room. Carter was looking down, pretending to study his curriculum, when he noticed Adam Proffit taking what seemed like a deliberately long time walking to the door. Carter looked up and found the young man staring at him.

"Can I help you with something?" Carter asked rather formally.

"Uh, no, thanks, Professor. I enjoyed your class. It's good to have you here."

"Thank you," Carter replied. "It's good to be here. And, by the way, I was very impressed by your performance today. Good work."

"Thanks," Adam replied looking bashfully down at his feet and then, after glancing at Carter once last time, disappeared from the room.

As soon as Adam left the room, Carter's stomach convulsed, and he closed his mouth tightly just in time to prevent the vomit that had ejected from his stomach from pouring out. It burned as he swallowed, and he rushed down the hall to the faculty men's room, where he rinsed out his mouth and splashed his face with cool water.

CHAPTER 4

▼

IS HE?

That was intense, Adam thought as he walked out of the English 601 classroom. *I know it wasn't just me. He had to feel it too. I know he had to.*

It was Adam's fourth and final year at Melbourne, and he had done a thorough job of hiding his sexuality from the other boys. He was a star cross-country runner, played senior lacrosse and soccer, and was even roommates with Kellum Thurman, a prefect. Adam had developed a crush on Kellum during his Fourth Form year. While Adam had secretly hoped that Kellum might be gay, these hopes had not materialized. At least, Kellum had never given Adam any solid indication that the attraction might be mutual, and Adam dared not do anything to reveal his true feelings.

As far as Adam knew, no student had ever been exposed as a homosexual at Melbourne. But he was certain that any such revelation would not go over well in the conservatively charged environment of the school. Adam was sure that the discovery of who he really was would lead to his expulsion or at least to a strong request that he withdraw from the school. After all, students with strong ties to the school had been expelled or asked to leave for a lot less. These even included fourth- and fifth-generation legacy students, some of whose last names appeared on buildings scattered across the campus. Melbourne had little tolerance for students who failed to conform to its high standards. Even the tiniest infraction of the Honor Code was grounds for expulsion. And although it was not written,

Adam was certain that being gay would not fit within the rigid moral guidelines expected of Melbourne men.

There were a few other students whom Adam suspected might be gay, but in the repressive atmosphere of the school, they were undoubtedly just as terrified as he was of having their secrets known. There were a few others who, perhaps, spent too long glancing at classmates in the locker rooms and who rarely attended the "mixers" that provided opportunities to get together and mingle with girls from the surrounding prep schools. Then there were a few students whom everyone assumed were gay, who all roomed with one another, and whom the other students avoided like lepers for fear of even the most remote association. But as long as there was no concrete proof of an impropriety, these students went about their business under the more or less unspoken edict of "don't ask, don't tell," much like the environment in the military.

At least they get left alone, Adam often thought, remembering the long, torturous days of attending the coed day school where male-female politics seemed to bring out the worst and most cruel behaviors in his classmates. It had been in day school that Adam had worked hard to perfect a mask to hide who he really was, although he had never been able to completely dispel speculation about his sexual orientation. He had been relieved, when he first arrived at Melbourne, that no one from his former school was in the student body, giving him the chance to break free from the past. As it turned out, he had become well liked and had excelled in both sports and academics.

Whenever Adam sensed a mutual attraction to another student, he did his best to shrug it off, telling himself not to fall prey to the overactive libidos of the other boys, who, but for their isolation from the opposite sex, would never have entertained the slightest curiosity about sexual intimacy with another guy. *Boarding school has a way of fucking with Mr. Kinsey's scale*, Adam sometimes thought. He had read that boarding school students' behavior was not unlike that of prisoners who engaged in homosexual conduct while in prison but returned to heterosexual activity as soon as they were back on the street.

But what Adam had felt in Professor Moran's presence was much stronger than anything he had ever experienced before. The attraction was not the reaction of a student so horny that he might—at least, on this occasion—let another guy help him out. Adam sensed that Professor Moran knew who he was and what he was, even if the fact that Adam was a student made him uncomfortable. Or maybe he was just put off by Adam's apparent suspicions. But whatever suspicion or knowledge, or even curious attraction, that the new professor might have, there was far too much at stake to risk acting upon it—at least, not without the most extreme caution.

CHAPTER 5

▼

KELLUM

"Hey, what ya reading?" Kellum Thurman said as he walked into the dormitory room he shared with Adam.

Like most of the rooms at Melbourne, the walls of Adam and Kellum's room were lined with clutter—sports memorabilia, street signs, the obligatory poster of a hot supermodel in a wet swimsuit, hubcaps, license plates, and many other pieces of junk that qualified as cool to students of their age. The more exotic the clutter, the cooler the dorm room. Their room also contained two reclining chairs of not-too-recent vintage, heavily worn, with stuffing poking from the armrests. Aside from high-end stereo equipment, an ugly but comfortable reclining chair was among the most coveted possessions in a Melbourne dorm room. The most hideous, most tattered chairs were often passed down from graduating Six Formers to lower classmen who were cool enough to have close friends among the Sixth Form. The provenance of one's reclining chair could, therefore, provide an additional layer of prestige. All the dormitory rooms had oak bunk beds that could be taken apart to form two singles or left as a bunk in rooms like Adam and Kellum's that were too filled with junk to permit any other configuration.

Kellum had just returned from the shower and continued to dry off as Adam watched from the corner of his eye, admiring the architectural perfection of Kellum's body—his smooth, tan skin, straight black hair, and rippling musculature. But as he secretly watched Kellum drying himself with his towel, Adam realized that the crush he had always felt for Kellum somehow had slightly less of a hold over him.

He thought about all the times he had watched Kellum dress and undress. There had been a few occasions when Kellum had even noticed, prompting laughter and a comment of, "What are you looking at, you homo?" Adam would usually retort, "Just your scrawny, lily-white ass, you pussy." They would both laugh, and that would be the end of it.

This time, watching Kellum pull up his boxer shorts, Adam was relieved not to feel such an intense attraction to him, even if he still admired Kellum's athletic build. Adam's infatuation had suddenly shifted from Kellum to someone with whom—at least, he hoped—he might have some chance of making a personal and physical connection, if only because there seemed to be some kind of dynamic pull between them, even if he was unsure what it was or what it might mean, if anything. But the distraction from his ordinary feelings for Kellum somehow felt reassuring to Adam, a slight break away from the complex, unrequited feelings that had for so long burdened their friendship.

"I said, what you reading?" Kellum repeated, a little irritably.

"Oh, just trying to get ahead in English. Hey, do you have Professor Moran too?"

"No, I've got Brumfield, cranky old bastard."

While cursing was not generally permitted at Melbourne and would quickly land anyone in demerit hall, this rule did not apply within the privacy of the dormitory rooms, where even the prefects like Kellum Thurman disgorged foul language with a fluency that could make a five-dollar hooker blush.

"You have my sympathies. I had him first year. He'd sooner give you a fucking demerit than look at you sideways."

"I know. I think he must have given me fifteen demerits first year for not having my shirt tucked in. I practically spent the whole damn year in demerit hall."

Demerits were another component of the controls on conduct imposed on the students at Melbourne. Five or more demerits landed a student in demerit hall on Saturday night, which, aside from Friday night, was the only evening of the week when mandatory study times were not imposed. This meant missing whatever movies might be playing in the Fine Arts Building, usually old black-and-white releases or other more current films that were considered high caliber. If a student received an excessive number of demerits, he might be asked to leave the school. But such a case would have been extremely rare, because expulsions were usually restricted to Honor Code violations rather than the petty behavioral violations for which demerits were given. If a student received more than twenty demerits, he could work them off by attending demerit hall and by performing odd jobs for faculty, such as washing their cars or working in their gardens. While Sixth Form students, like faculty, were entitled to issue demerits, it was generally considered uncool of them to do so, unless the person in question was too cocky or otherwise deserved comeuppance.

"So, you've got Moran. Lucky bastard. Moran seems like a really nice guy. A little quiet, though, and God knows he doesn't look much older than we are."

"Yeah, I know. I think he's barely out of college and finished early. Heard he's only here for a year, and then he's got some really prestigious fellowship at Harvard."

"Sweet," Kellum said. "Guess he can show me around when I get there next year."

"Cocky bastard," Adam replied. "Guess I'd be pretty fucking confident, too, if I had a foundation behind my name. Rich bastard."

"Yeah, sucks to be me. Hey, you still thinking about Vandy?" Kellum said, changing the subject.

"Yeah, I'm thinking about it. Just not sure. The old man is telling me I have to get into Duke, 'cause that's where he always wanted to go. Not that it would suck, but part of me would really like to go up east or maybe even out west, like Stanford. Besides, I don't know why I would even need to go to college if I work for the old man. I'm not sure you really need a college degree to be a fast-food distributor."

"Little dissension in the ranks?"

"I'm not putting him down. I mean, he's done really well…"

"Yeah, I hear those guys make a dime for every freaking hamburger or Coke that's sold, and that's a bloody fortune."

"Well, I don't think we'll ever have a foundation like Mister Rockefeller, but he does OK. I think I wanna do something different. Just not sure yet what it is."

"With your fucking grades, you should be able to get into anywhere and do whatever you want."

"Yeah, just think. If we could combine my grades and your fucking money, I could be president."

"Maybe we should make a baby?" Kellum said, laughing, "Bend over and show me that fine pussy of yours."

"Fucking asshole," Adam said, throwing the pillow from behind his head at Kellum, who ducked as it grazed him on his shoulder. It was that kind of comment that used to drive Adam wild with lust, causing him to wonder whether

Kellum knew how he really felt, whether Kellum wanted him the same way, or whether Kellum would reject him.

The only thing Adam could do to clear his head of the confusion was go to the bathroom and jack off. But this time, Adam just laughed at what Kellum had said because he thought it was funny, that it was perhaps nothing more than a brassy comment from his roommate that had no hidden meanings whatsoever. Adam felt liberated that the comment failed to send him into the emotional tailspin he had fallen into the other times Kellum had made lewd comments implying that Adam was his woman. Referring to one's classmates with feminine pronouns was one of the highest forms of pejorative at Melbourne.

"I'm gonna get a few minutes of shut-eye before dinner," Adam said. "Mind grabbing the light—and hey, could you toss me my pillow?"

"Sure," Kellum said, throwing Adam's pillow before turning off the light and closing the door.

Adam turned over on his stomach, laid his head on his pillow, and thought about what it would feel like to be held by Professor Moran. For the first time since Adam had arrived at Melbourne, he felt that he could be normal and that perhaps the object of his attraction was someone like him, for whom his feelings would not provide a basis for disgust, revulsion, or rejection.

CHAPTER 6

▼

SO FAR, SO GOOD

Carter taught his remaining classes that day without incident, trying to keep his mind off of what had happened earlier, trying to convince himself that nothing had happened at all. *Just the workings of an overactive imagination*, he thought. He enjoyed meeting the rest of the students he would be teaching that semester. They were even better prepared and more engaged in their work than many of the undergraduates he had taught during his master's program.

After his last class, he walked along the brick paths that led to the various buildings on campus. The students spoke to him as they passed, and Carter could see why the other teachers enjoyed the collegiate atmosphere of the school. But he realized that things would never work out for him if he returned here as a teacher after his Harvard studies, that a gay faculty member would not fit in. Jake Sommerville had already made it clear that "fruits" could not be trusted around the students. Carter wondered whether Jake was right. The events of the morning were perhaps proof enough. *Hell*, he thought, *I'll bet I'm only four years older than he is—and besides, nothing happened, and nothing will happen.*

Although Carter had acknowledged his sexuality, he had not even begun to reconcile how it might fit in with his other values. By accepting that he was gay, he had already broken away from social convention, and he understood that some societal norms needed to be broken. But his reaction to Adam Proffit was not one of them. No matter how close in age they were, he was still the teacher, and Adam was the student. As far as Carter was concerned, even if there was an attraction between them, it could not go anywhere, and that would be the end of it.

*   *   *   *

It was almost six thirty in the evening. Carter was running late for dinner. He locked his apartment and scurried down the stairs to the main dining hall, where he walked to the table at which he was to be the presiding faculty member.

Every Monday, Wednesday, and Thursday evening, the students were assigned to certain dinner tables at which their attendance was mandatory. Each table was presided over by a faculty member—and his wife, if he was married. The few female faculty members on staff were married to other male faculty. The seating assignments were rotated every two weeks, and on Sunday evenings, the students were required to sit with their faculty advisors.

The students stood up from their chairs when Carter reached the table.

"Please, gentleman, take your seats."

Several "thank you, sir's" were mumbled across the table, and everyone sat down. The school chaplain, who was seated across the dining room, stood to give an invocation. Although Melbourne touted itself as nondenominational, the chaplain was and always had been Episcopalian.

As soon as the blessing was finished, Third Form students in white jackets rushed trays of food to each table. At Melbourne, all Third Form students were required to work as waiters for at least four weeks during the academic year. Unlike other schools, where these positions were filled by hired staff or students on financial aid, even the wealthiest students at Melbourne had to fulfill this requirement, which was part of the egalitarian ethos of the school. While, for some students, having their names emblazoned across the buildings seemed to undermine the ideal that all Melbourne students were equal, all the students agreed on their universal hatred of having to wait tables. The constant jibes from other students who had already completed their waiting requirement only made the task less pleasant. But although some of the students genuinely considered the task beneath them, most of them accepted the obligation for what it was— another rite of passage to becoming a Melbourne man.

"Well," Carter said as he looked across the table at the students from each of the four Forms, "I believe I've met Mr. Donahue, but I haven't had the pleasure of meeting the rest of you. Why don't you go around the table and each tell me your name, what Form you're in, and where you're from."

Carter had read *Goodbye, Mr. Chips* more than once and envied the relationship that Mr. Chips had with his students. He admired the closeness and camaraderie that Mr. Chips shared with them and for which only the boarding school environment seemed conducive. However, Carter realized that his sexuality presented a legitimate obstacle to gaining the venerated status of Mr. Chips, although he sometimes mused about rewriting the story to present Mr. Chips as something of a British dandy who, in the film version, would be played by Sir Ian McKellan.

Each of the students stated the information requested. Then one of the students asked, "Professor Moran, where are you from?"

"I'm from Mississippi. South Mississippi."

"You mean the Delta?" another student asked.

"No, nowhere that civilized," Carter quipped. His remark met with smiles by a few of the students.

"You don't have much of an accent," another student commented.

"No, that was beaten out of me at a young age. You know, mamma, *whap*, mamma, *whap*," Carter repeated in his best redneck accent, followed by a polite "Mother," which he pronounced with only the faintest hint of the southern cadence, of which he had worked so hard to rid himself. This comment was followed by laughter from the students, who were not used to the informality with which Carter spoke to them.

"So, Professor Moran, you're not married?"

"No, I'm not."

"Well, do your best to stay away from the Fauquier County girls. Real pack of dogs," another student retorted, followed by hushed laughter from the others.

"Isn't your mother from Fauquier County, Leyton?" another student remarked. "Yeah, your eyes are kind of droopy too, arf, arf."

Carter smiled and thought to himself, *So far, so good.*

CHAPTER 7

▼

WUTHERING HEIGHTS

Adam looked forward to each English class with Professor Moran with great anticipation. He liked to watch Professor Moran walk around the room, the way the contours of his shape became defined through his clothes when he reached to the top of the blackboard. He noticed the very slight beginnings of a receding hairline, and imagined what Professor Moran would look like as his hair thinned. Adam remembered his father's financial advisor, who came to the Proffits' house every once in a while to review his father's portfolio. He was probably in his thirties, and Adam had noticed that he never wore a wedding ring. He was losing his blond hair, which he kept short and clean-cut, and which Adam thought looked very lawyerlike and distinguished. Adam always made a point of answering the door whenever he came to the house. He looked forward to the momentary physical contact of shaking his hand. It took so little to run his sexual turbines.

There had been one occasion at camp, in the mountains of Georgia, when one of the other boys in his cabin dared Adam to pull his pants down. "Come on," the boy had said. "I'll do it if you do it." Adam agreed with great reluctance and excitement. He and the other boy pulled their shorts down.

"Go ahead, touch it," the other boy instructed, pointing at his own penis.

"No," Adam replied, afraid that it was some kind of trick.

The other boy grabbed Adam's hand and placed it on his penis, moving Adam's hand back and forth until Adam completed the job without further provocation. Then it was his turn. The other boy seemed to know what he was doing and finished his work more quickly than Adam had. Adam was on cloud nine—at least until the next morning, when the other boy would not even look at him, much less speak to him. Before long, the other boy started calling Adam a faggot and whispering to the other boys whenever Adam passed by. For the remaining four weeks of camp, he had become an untouchable. None of the other boys spoke to him unless they had to, and before long the girls started doing the same. It was the last time Adam had ever had any kind of sexual contact with anyone. And whenever he felt tempted to act upon his attractions, he remembered the experience at camp, the extreme loneliness and isolation, and the feeling that he just wanted to die.

"And, Mr. Proffit, why don't you enlighten us with a description of the classical and romantic imagery of the two settings created by Ms. Brontë and Ms. Austin?"

Professor Moran had finally called on Adam again, although whenever Adam spoke it seemed as if Professor Moran was trying hard not to listen, as if calling upon him was only out of obligation or an attempt not to make his avoidance of Adam seem conspicuous—at least, not to the other students. But it was obvious to Adam.

"Well," Adam began, "the setting in *Wuthering Heights* is highly romantic. Wuthering Heights, as its name suggests, is a wild and contemptuous place. The architecture is gothic and foreboding, which creates an immediate sense of mystery and suspicion. In contrast, Mr. Darcy's Pemberley is a classic English country house, with formal gardens and well-manicured grounds, probably inspired by Capability Brown. The atmosphere of Pemberley suggests that everything taking place inside is as well mannered and balanced as the place itself."

When Adam finished, even the other students were impressed by the answer he had given. And despite Professor Moran's best efforts to overlook Adam, the student had clearly captured his attention.

"Uh, well, Mr. Proffit, excellent job."

One of the other students looked over at Adam to catch his attention. Underneath his desk, he motioned his hand as if masturbating. It was the universal symbol for brownnosing. But this was one occasion when the jibes about being a brainiac did not bother Adam. Professor Moran had noticed him, and Adam was certain he was impressed.

"OK then, class, papers are due next Friday, and I hope all of you will give as much attention to the work as Mr. Proffit has. Don't disappoint me."

This comment prompted yet another student to poke his tongue into his cheek, which was the symbol for a suck job.

"Way to go, Proffit," Holder Colomb said as they left the classroom. "Way to make everyone else look like we've got numb nuts."

"Aw, fuck you, Colomb. You don't need any help with that. Maybe if you spent less time jacking off and more time studying, you'd get an answer right once in a while too."

"That's pretty funny," Kellum Thurman said, having overheard the comment as he jogged through the hall to catch up with Adam. "Yeah, Colomb, it might help your eyesight and those hairy palms too. Dude, it's called Nair. You use it on your pussy. Maybe you should try it on your palms."

"Funny, Thurman. But your mom used it all up before I did her last night."

"My mother's got better taste than that, Colomb. You must have had her confused with your own mom."

"Good one, Thurman," Holder conceded, acquiescing to having lost the round.

No matter what the subject of the insults or sarcasm, such conversations invariably turned to one's mother, her anatomy, or the perverse sexual acts she could perform.

CHAPTER 8

▼

RULES OF ENGAGEMENT

Carter remained at his desk after his class was dismissed. He felt better than he had in a long time. For the past weeks, he had been avoiding any eye contact or discussion with Adam Proffit. Carter realized how unfair his treatment had been to Adam. But he did not want to encourage the boy in any way if there really was an attraction between them, and he was terrified of how his own emotions might overpower him as well.

Today, finally, Carter had called on Adam, and when Adam delivered his well-spoken answer to Carter's question, Carter began to feel at ease. Whatever had overcome him the last time this student had spoken in class had apparently dissipated, and Carter was simply able to admire the student for what he was—a handsome, extremely bright, and sensitive member of the Melbourne student body.

Carter sensed, however, that Adam was attracted to him. Carter thought of his own behavior when he was Adam Proffit's age and how he was still suppressing his feelings for other men. *Adam is much more evolved at his age than I was*, Carter thought, knowing that he had still not come to terms with himself completely. When he was in college, he had found it much easier to avoid his feelings because he was so busy with his work-study job and his classes. Only now, however, the greater leisure time he had at Melbourne provided him with the opportunity to look for the answers to his many questions about who he was and who he wanted to become.

Carter was roused from his thoughts by a knock at the classroom door.

"Professor Moran, do you have a moment?"

Carter looked up and saw Adam Proffit standing in the doorway. As relieved as he had felt that his ostensible attraction to this student had abated, the prospect of a one-on-one discussion with him made Carter uneasy.

"Uh, sure, Mr. Proffit. Please come in."

Adam shut the door behind him, and Carter watched as he walked into the room almost sheepishly, lacking the casual confidence of his usual stride. Carter wondered what Adam Proffit could possibly have to discuss with him that would require closing the door, praying that the occasion would not be to confess his feelings. After all, he had only just been able to call on the student and, now, to speak calmly with him, but he was certainly not ready for any personal subjects that Adam Proffit might raise.

Adam pulled up a chair to the side of Carter's desk. Carter fidgeted nervously with his papers, pretending to organize them, even though they did not need it.

"Um, Professor Moran, I wanted to talk to you about becoming my faculty advisor. Professor McCullough has been my faculty advisor for my first three years, but he is on sabbatical this year, and so they assigned me to Professor Caruthers, the French teacher. Anyway, I don't know Professor Caruthers at all, and I wanted to know if you'd consider being my faculty advisor. I checked with Mrs. Brockman already, and she said you have a space open. It's just that I'm going to be making a lot of big decisions this year, about college and all, and I need someone I can really talk to. I thought maybe you would be a good person."

Adam observed the concerned, almost pensive look that came across his professor's face and wondered whether he was making a big mistake, whether his emotions were causing him to make unfounded, possibly disastrous, decisions.

Carter was both relieved and unnerved by the request. He felt flattered that Adam Proffit felt an affinity for him, but at the same time he was concerned that the affinity could be the result of a crush.

"But you don't really know me any better than Professor Caruthers," Carter said, and, noticing the immediate crestfallen look on Adam's face, he continued. "I mean, don't get me wrong. I'm flattered you asked. But I haven't been here long, and I'm not really experienced at being a faculty advisor. I can't give you the best advice about going to or getting into college."

"You got into Harvard, didn't you?" Adam asked a little defensively.

"Oh, yes, I did," Carter responded, a little uplifted, unused to feeling proud of his accomplishments. In some ways, he was still the shy, quiet boy his father used to beat whenever he had too much beer or whiskey. "I meant, there are other teachers here with a lot more experience than me and whom you probably already know better than you know me."

"I understand if you don't want to," Adam sighed. He looked devastated.

"No, it's not that at all. I'd be honored and flattered to be your faculty advisor. I just want to make sure that you know what you're getting. As you said yourself, you're going to be making some terrifically important decisions this year, and you want the best counseling and advice you can get when you make them."

"I'm sure I'd like to have you as my faculty advisor," Adam said, trying to smile but looking like he might also burst into tears.

"Wonderful, then. Consider it done." As soon as the words came from Carter's mouth, he began to regret them. He wished that he had lied or invented some plausible excuse that would have allowed him to decline the request gently, without making it seem like a rejection. But nothing had come to mind.

"Thank you, sir," Adam said, standing, extending his hand.

Their hands touched in their first physical contact with each other. For both, it was overpowering. Adam grasped Carter's hand more firmly, more tightly, as if that solitary handshake had become a substitute for holding each other closely, safe from all judgment and ridicule. Carter had no idea how long the handshake lasted, probably no more than a few seconds, but the sheer volume of information communicated between him and Adam during the brief contact seemed to suggest otherwise. Carter almost felt that each of them suddenly understood the lifetime—however brief to date—of sorrow, fear, disappointment, loneliness, and pain that the other had experienced.

Carter stood as their hands remained clasped and then released his grip. He felt faint, dizzy, and exhausted. He needed to catch his breath.

"Thanks, Professor Moran. You won't regret this," Adam said.

I hope I don't regret this, Carter thought as Adam disappeared from the room. Carter placed his hands on his forehead and ran his fingers tightly down his face to try to release the mounting tension in his head. "Just seven more months," he whispered to himself. "Just seven more months, and then you're out of here."

CHAPTER 9

▼

THE RAPP

"You're in a good mood," Kellum said, looking up from a book as Adam walked into their dorm room.

"Yeah," Adam smiled. "I am."

"What's the occasion? You look like you just got laid."

"No occasion, really. I just talked to Professor Moran about becoming my faculty advisor, that's all."

"Don't blame you for switching from Caruthers. What a goddamn creep, all that fucking dandruff."

"I know. And I think Professor Moran can really help me decide about college, maybe even help smooth things over with my dad if I don't go to Duke."

"That'd be great, but don't you think you're putting a little too much confidence in this guy? He hasn't been here long. I mean, I know he's going to Harvard and all, but d'ya think your expectations might be a little too high?"

"I'm not like you," Adam responded defensively. "I don't have every university knocking at my door 'cause they want my family to give 'em a million bucks."

"Fuck you, Proffit. I've worked my ass off here. You don't become a prefect by sitting on your ass. And no, you're not like me. I have to kill myself for the grades I get. They come easy to you. And how would you like it if everybody, even your best friend, assumed the only reason you ever accomplished anything was because your family has money?"

"I'm sorry," Adam said, sensing how deeply Kellum had been wounded by the comment, but at the same time feeling blown away that Kellum considered him his best friend. While Adam thought of Kellum as his closest friend, both in and out of Melbourne, Kellum was so well liked and admired by everyone that Adam had never thought Kellum held him in such high regard.

"I really am sorry," Adam continued. "I was being a dick. I'm just stressed out about the whole college thing, about trying to deal with my dad, with knowing that if I don't go to Duke, I'm probably going to need a full scholarship 'cause the old man won't pay for it otherwise. That really limits my options, ya know. It's one thing to get into Stanford or Yale. It's another thing to pay for it. And I'm sure I won't qualify for financial aid. So, whatever scholarships I get will have to be purely academic."

"You never told me your dad wouldn't pay if you don't go to Duke. What a dick. What about a track scholarship? You can run your nuts off."

"I'm not a bad runner as far as the prep league goes, but in terms of competing nationally, I don't think I'd rank that high. I might be able to get a combination academic and athletic scholarship. It just limits where I can go."

"Can't you borrow the money? Get a student loan or something?"

"I won't likely qualify, thanks to the fast-food king."

"Shit, Proffit. I didn't know. Damn. I mean, crap. Hey, you know what, if you get in where you want to go, I'll loan you the money. Fuck, I'll give you the money. It's only money. What are friends for?"

Adam was speechless. Kellum had not only admitted that he considered Adam his closest friend but was willing to commit to funding Adam's education. It was too much. Adam resisted the slight urge to pursue the offer further, to ask whether Kellum really had that kind of control over his finances. He knew he could never take a penny from Kellum, anyway. He still had a hard time believing he and Kellum were roommates, much less good friends. Kellum was not only the all-American, quintessential jock but also good-looking, intelligent, popular, and one of the richest and most genuine guys at Melbourne. Everyone, both faculty and students, liked Kellum, who, despite everything he had going for him, was genuinely kind to everyone. He could make others feel good about themselves just because he had taken the time to talk to them.

"Hey, want to go to the Rapp and get a burger and shake? My treat?" Adam asked, wanting to extend some measure of generosity, even if it was only a token in comparison to the gesture that Kellum had just made.

The Rapp was short for the Rappahannock Grill, named for the Rappahannock River, which surrounded parts of the school. It was open every day of the week and closed only during mandatory dinners in the main dining hall. Unlike the student commissary—where all students were required to have a charge account so their books, supplies, and athletic gear could be billed to their parents—the Rapp took only cash, which the students rarely kept in abundance, because most parents who sent their children to Melbourne did not want them corrupted by having access to substantial amounts of currency.

Not having ready cash prompted some students to begin various business endeavors, such as Saturday and Sunday doughnut deliveries to the dorm rooms or even weekend newspaper routes. The administration encouraged such activities because the school took pride in fostering the entrepreneurial spirit. Of course, there were some students, with perhaps less command of industry, who found ways to produce extra cash—students such as Eduardo Montoya, the Argentine student who charged almost anything he could to his parents' account in the commissary. He would then sell the merchandise to other students for cash at drastically reduced prices. His specialty was high-end athletic equipment such as tennis rackets and expensive tennis shoes, for which his parents paid without a murmur. While the administration probably would have considered the enterprise an Honor Code violation if they had ever learned of it, the Montoya family owned more than half the hotels in Argentina. And Eduardo's dozens of happy customers were too pleased with the comfortable prices of his products to register any complaints.

CHAPTER 10

▼

PARENTS' WEEKEND

During the annual Parents' Weekend, the mothers and fathers, extended family, and any other relations were invited to the Melbourne School for a series of receptions, parties, lectures, and meetings with professors and faculty advisors. The weekend provided an opportunity, particularly for the parents of new students, to see for themselves how their sons were doing. The weekend also provided an important marketing opportunity for the school to show that the thirty-plus-thousand-dollar tuition was being well spent. During this time, school administrators were eager to meet with parents who had made or might make donations to the school, and to encourage other parents to send their younger sons to Melbourne as well. Following all the receptions, parties, and meetings, parents took their children away for the remainder of the weekend—usually to Washington DC, Richmond, or even Charlottesville—to spend time together away from the school.

*   *   *   *

During his Third Form year, Adam had been the only student whose parents had not come for Parents' Weekend. They were in Paris. After the receptions had ended, all the other students left with their parents, making the campus seem desolate, possibly one of the loneliest places Adam had ever been. Even the faculty was out of sight, having left campus or choosing to rest in their private quarters after the mixing and mingling with parents.

When Kellum had returned with his parents, his mother held Adam's hand in both of hers. "If only I had known your parents weren't coming, we would have taken you with us," she'd apologized in her lovely southern drawl.

Kellum's mother was beautiful. She had dark black hair, the same as Kellum's, which she wore behind her ears. She was casually but fashionably dressed as though she had just walked off the cover of *Town & Country* magazine—perfectly tanned, coiffed, and manicured, completely relaxed and content.

"Oh, that's OK." Adam tried to seem cheerful about it.

"Well, it's not OK at all. Next year, if your parents don't come, you're coming with us!"

"Thank you, Mrs. Thurman, that would be great," Adam had replied, not altogether certain whether Kellum would have extended the invitation if it had been up to him. But Adam thought there would at least be enough time for Kellum and the Thurmans to politely forget that the offer had been made if Kellum did not want him to go with them.

Much to Adam's surprise, Kellum had stopped by his dormitory room several days before the next Parents' Weekend and asked whether Adam's parents would be coming that year.

"Nope," Adam had replied, remembering Mrs. Thurman's invitation but not daring to bring it up.

"Then you're coming with us," Kellum had begun. "No two ways about it. I could use the company, and besides, my mother will never let me hear the end of it if you don't come. So that's that, all right?"

"OK. Thanks, Kellum."

"Don't mention it. Just remember to bring at least a jacket and a few ties. Mother always likes to hit the good restaurants when they're up here."

"I will, thanks. Thanks a lot."

"Yup," Kellum had replied nonchalantly. "See you later."

At first the idea of staying with the Thurmans had made Adam nervous. Rumors had circulated the first week Adam arrived at Melbourne that Kellum's parents were building a new wing for the school's library. The rumors quickly materialized into reality when bulldozers arrived several weeks later, followed by a modest sign that read, "Future Site of the Drummond E. Thurman Library Wing," named after Kellum's grandfather, a 1937 graduate of the Melbourne School.

While Adam's family fell somewhere near the lower end of the upper middle classes, the social circle his parents kept never included people like the Thurmans. Adam's father worked long hours, and when he was not working, he and Adam's stepmother were either traveling or entertaining themselves with other people who, like them, had made the leap from the lower middle class into the bottom reaches of the upper middle class. These were people with second and even third homes, expensive cars, and fine clothes, but not the kind of money that built wings onto libraries.

Adam was again surprised, and pleasantly so, that the Thurmans seemed far more down-to-earth than his own father and stepmother were. Kellum's parents took a genuine interest in Adam and asked what classes he enjoyed and what his hopes were for the future.

"Kellum tells me you're at the top of your class, probably going to be valedictorian?" Mrs. Thurman said over dinner in the Lafayette Room of the Hay-Adams Hotel, where they were staying.

"Well, I don't know about that," Adam responded bashfully, surprised that Kellum had known enough about how well or poorly he had been doing in his classes to pass the information along to his family.

"He also tells me you're quite a good runner," Mrs. Thurman continued, noticing that Adam was becoming embarrassed by the attention. Other school rumors had disclosed that Kellum's mother was from Savannah, Georgia, and that her family was even richer than the Thurmans. None of this mattered to Adam, who thought Mrs. Thurman was the nicest and most beautiful woman he had ever met. She was the kind of woman who made Adam wish even more that he were straight, which would make everything so much easier. Then he could simply enjoy being friends with Kellum instead of being tortured by his feelings for him.

That evening Kellum and Adam had stayed in the same room, down the hall from Kellum's parents.

"So, what d'ya think of the folks?" Kellum asked as he stepped out of his shoes and loosened his tie.

"They're amazing, Kellum. You're really lucky. I've never met such nice people in my whole life, really."

"Yeah, they're pretty awesome," Kellum responded almost sadly, as if there were something more to the picture of the Thurman family than met the eye. Adam sensed there were no dark secrets in the Thurmans' closets. The Thurmans were too kind and genuine for anything like that. Adam thought about the compliments he had been given at dinner, particularly about his academic record.

While the Thurmans were undoubtedly proud of Kellum, Adam sensed the great pressure Kellum placed on himself to measure up, if not to the Thurmans' expectations of him, then to the expectations Kellum established for himself. *It would be easy to disappoint parents who are assholes*, Adam thought. He imagined how living up to the unspoken standards of the Thurmans was probably more difficult than he had ever considered.

"So, what do ya say we check out the pay-per-view?" Kellum asked as he unbuttoned his shirt and then dropped his pants. Adam could not help noticing Kellum's penis, which had flopped out the front flap of his boxer shorts.

"Oops," Kellum said, shoving it back into his boxers. "Didn't mean to advertise my business."

"You're a nut," Adam said, laughing, excited by what he had seen.

"Well, let's see what kind of snacks we've got in the honor bar," Kellum suggested.

While drinking was prohibited on campus and would have been grounds for expulsion, the rule did not apply when students had checked out for the weekend. Except for Parents' Weekend, leaving the school for a weekend was a privilege reserved for upperclassmen, who could leave campus four times a year and miss Saturday classes.

"Here, how about a Heiny?" Kellum said, tossing a cold beer from the honor bar to Adam.

I'd like a heinie, Adam thought, admiring Kellum's rear end as he bent over, looking into the honor bar. "Thanks," Adam replied.

After the weekend with Kellum and his parents, Adam and Kellum spent more and more time together. By the end of the year, Kellum had asked Adam to be his roommate, to which Adam promptly agreed. They had been roommates ever since.

CHAPTER 11

▼

LIGHTS-OUT

The Thurmans did not come for Parents' Weekend this year, but parents of Sixth Form students almost never did. During the Fifth and Sixth Form years, many of the upperclassmen left campus unchaperoned during Parents' Weekend. Most went to Washington DC, and some went to Charlottesville to party with the University of Virginia crowd.

"What do you want to do for Parents' Weekend?" Kellum had asked.

"I don't know. Got any ideas?"

"Yeah, Mother offered us a room at the Hay-Adams, but I talked to her about New York instead. What do ya think?"

"I can't really afford to go to New York. How about going to Charlottesville?"

"Hell, Adam, it's on Big Momma. So don't worry about the damn cost, OK?"

"Um, well, if you say so," Adam replied, although he felt awkward always being on the receiving end of the Thurmans' generosity.

"Cool," Kellum said, "'cause I spoke with Tilda, and she and a couple of her girlfriends might meet us up there."

Matilda Thurman, known to her friends as Tilda, was Kellum's older sister and a freshman at Vassar. Before going to college, Tilda had attended one of the nearby girls' schools whose students interacted socially during sponsored events, such as mixers, with the boys from Melbourne. Adam remembered the first time Kellum introduced him to Tilda during one of the fall mixers.

"God, don't ya love mixers," Tilda had said with the same gorgeous southern drawl as her mother. "Sounds like drinks."

Adam had suspected immediately that Tilda was the wild member of the Thurman clan, completely uninhibited by the expectations that haunted Kellum. She was young, beautiful, and rich, not restrained by any unspoken expectations. Nothing would stop her from having a good time.

"Sounds like fun," Adam replied. "How is Tilda?"

"She's doin' great. But you know Tilda: she could turn a prostate exam into a party."

"You really need help, ya know that?" Adam said laughing.

"That's what they tell me. Anyway, we'll leave right after class Friday. It'll be great."

*   *   *   *

It had been lights-out for at least twenty minutes. Adam lay awake in bed. He could hear Kellum breathing deeply, as he always did after he fell asleep. Adam closed his eyes and began narrating the fantasy for which he had imagined every detail. It always began the same way.

*   *   *   *

Adam knocked at the door to Professor Moran's apartment with his term paper and notes in hand. He was dressed for the occasion in the white linen shirt and shorts he had bought at Banana Republic on his last trip to DC.

"What is it?" Professor Moran asked when he opened the door.

"Sorry to bother you, Professor, but I wanted to see if you might have a few minutes to go over my term paper," was Adam's prepared response.

"It's Friday night. Can't this wait until Monday?"

"Well, I wanted to try and get ahead on it this weekend. I'll take only a few minutes, I promise."

"Well, OK. Come in."

Adam followed Professor Moran into his apartment. He watched as the professor walked down the hall wearing an Ole Miss T-shirt and a faded pair of cotton athletic shorts. His legs were more muscular than Adam had imagined. Adam admired the contours of his back, visible through the old T-shirt.

The professor led Adam into the narrow kitchen and said, "Have a seat. Would you like some coffee?"

"That'd be great. Black, please," Adam responded, placing his paper on the table. "I think I know where I'm going with this, but I wanted to get some advice about organization and about how far I should go into some of the issues."

"Well, let's see what you have," Professor Moran said, handing Adam a cup of coffee, from which Adam only took a small sip, leaving the rest in the cup to use later.

During a break in their discussion, Professor Moran left to go to the bathroom. Adam waited impatiently, nervously. But as the professor walked back into the kitchen, Adam poured the remaining contents of his coffee cup across the front of his shirt and shorts.

"Damn it!" Adam said loudly. "I'm sorry, Professor. I didn't mean to swear."

Professor Moran was frozen.

"Darn, these are going to stain if I don't rinse 'em right away. Do you mind?"

"Uh, well," Professor Moran replied unsuspectingly as Adam unbuttoned his shirt and then unzipped his shorts, which fell to the floor, leaving Adam standing naked in Professor Moran's kitchen. Professor Moran was speechless, not knowing what to do, afraid that someone might show up at his apartment.

Professor Moran left the room to gather something for Adam to wear and returned with a T-shirt and gym shorts. He found Adam rinsing the shorts and shirt in the sink. He stopped outside the threshold of the room, apparently to admire Adam's lean runner's build. His frame was narrower than the professor's but all muscle. Adam could hear Professor Moran's footfalls as he approached the kitchen and abruptly stopped at the doorway. Adam deliberately tensed his muscles as he rinsed his clothes, aware that he was being watched.

"Here you go," Professor Moran finally said, coming into the kitchen and handing Adam the clothes while trying to look in the other direction.

"Thanks, Professor. That sure was clumsy."

Adam threw the T-shirt over his shoulder and pulled the shorts up over his waist, but when he let go of the waistband, they were too large and fell to the floor.

"Uh," Professor Moran began, still speechless.

"No big deal. This shirt looks pretty big," Adam interjected, and he pulled the shirt over his shoulders deliberately slowly to give Professor Moran another chance to stare at him.

The shirt was just long enough so that Adam no longer looked naked.

"Hey, you know, Professor, *Wait Until Dark* is on tonight. In fact, it should be coming on in just a few minutes. Have you seen it?"

"You mean the old Audrey Hepburn movie?" Professor Moran replied, still stupefied.

"Yeah, that's the one. It's great. Anyway, everybody else is watching the game, so I'll never get a TV in the commons. Hey, do you want to see it? Where's your television?"

"Um, I have only one."

"Must be in the bedroom," Adam said as he walked out of the kitchen and toward the bedroom.

By the time Professor Moran caught up with him, Adam was lying on the bed with the television on and the lights off. Professor Moran turned on the lights. The bottom of Adam's T-shirt was beginning to ride up past his backside.

"Oh, come on, Professor," Adam said innocently. "This movie is really killer with the lights off. Do you mind?"

"Uh, no," Professor Moran replied and switched off the lights.

"Well, come on, sit down. It's just starting."

At this point in the dream, Professor Moran was powerless to do anything but obey Adam, who had no intention of leaving and who, in any event, could not be seen leaving in only a T-shirt. As the movie continued, Professor Moran began to relax more, becoming engrossed in the film. Adam gently nudged himself closer and closer to the professor until they were lying parallel across the bed.

They watched Audrey Hepburn, playing Susy Hendrix, pursued within the darkness of her apartment, giving her blind character a great advantage over her attacker. Adam startled on cue as Susy Hendrix evaded her assailant, pulling the T-shirt up a little higher as he stretched his buttocks into Professor Moran's crotch. Adam almost ejaculated as his bare skin made contact with the cotton of Professor's Moran's athletic shorts. Professor Moran did not move, paralyzed. Adam nudged himself more firmly into Professor Moran and could feel an erection forming against his backside, which caused Adam to grind into Professor Moran even harder. It seemed like only seconds before Professor Moran's clothes were off, and their bodies were enveloped in rapturous lovemaking, rubbing against each other, their tongues exploring each other's mouths as their hands moved with the same fluidity across each other's bodies.

*   *   *   *

"What the fuck?" Adam heard from the upper bunk. It was Kellum's voice, and Adam was back in the lower bunk of his room instead of in the arms of Professor Moran.

"Huh," Adam replied, pretending that he had just awakened from a violent dream. "Sorry, uh, nightmare."

"Well, keep it the fuck down, would ya?" Kellum said irritably. "I'm trying to sleep."

CHAPTER 12

▼

NEW YORK

Adam sat, gripping the armrest, lightly tapping his feet on the floor.

"Jittery enough?" Kellum asked as the plane began its final approach into JFK International Airport.

"Sorry, I'm pretty excited. I've never been to New York," Adam replied.

"What? Never been to New York? Man, are you in for the time of your life."

"I know. I can hardly wait. Please thank your parents again for me. I mean, I'll send them a note, of course, but just let 'em know how grateful I am."

"You know, Proffit, you worry too damn much. Of course I'll thank them for you. But it's no big deal, really. They're crazy about you."

It was a big deal to Adam, not just going to New York but going with Kellum. Despite his ongoing infatuation with Professor Moran, Adam still had strong feelings for Kellum. Adam could hardly imagine how anyone could not. Whether gay or straight, Kellum was one of those people that everyone was attracted to. In fact, Adam still had trouble believing that he and Kellum were such good friends. Being so close with the most popular guy in school was alien to Adam's experience, as he had been the shy kid that most of the girls had crushes on and most of the other guys avoided.

"Kellum," Tilda called out in her unmistakable southern accent as soon as Kellum and Adam stepped out of the deplaning area. Tilda was flanked by two equally beautiful girls.

"Oh, my God," Tilda continued as she hugged her brother affectionately. "And Adam, is that you? You keep getting better looking every time I see you." She gave Adam a big kiss on the lips. She and Kellum looked so much alike that, for a moment, Adam felt that he was kissing Kellum, and he tightened his lips around Tilda's a little more than he probably would have otherwise.

"Oh, and fresh too!" Tilda said as she pulled back gently, holding Adam's arms and studying him admiringly. "Well, let's get out of this dingy airport so we can start having some fun. But first, these are two friends I'd like you to meet. This is Mary Tate and Su Su. And this is my dashing brother, Kellum, and his handsome friend, Adam. Now remember, hands off, girls. These boys are still in high school. Keep it legal."

"Tilda, stop, please. You're embarrassing Adam," giggled Mary Tate.

"Oh, he's not embarrassed. He loves it. I can tell by the way he kissed me. You're gonna be a real heartbreaker, Adam Proffit, a real heartbreaker."

*   *   *   *

Tilda had the same effortless manner of putting people at ease as did the rest of the Thurmans. But her social ease, combined with her exuberant personality, probably made Tilda lethal to almost any man she had ever met. All other women must have seemed dull in comparison. Kellum had the same effect on people, Adam realized, and he wondered what type of people Tilda and Kellum would eventually marry, although he also wondered how anyone could measure up to the Thurmans.

"Do you all have any luggage?" Tilda asked.

"No, we carried everything on," Kellum replied.

"Good Lord, I could never make it as a man," Tilda said, eyeing their small suitcases. "Heck, my makeup case could hold more than what you two brought."

They piled into a taxi, and Tilda instructed the driver, "The Waldorf," she paused, then continued, "Astoria," anticipating the driver's apprehension as to which Waldorf she meant, the Waldorf-Astoria or the more expensive Waldorf Towers. But then, despite their great wealth, the Thurmans always traveled coach.

Seeing Kellum with Tilda made Adam feel much younger and less sophisticated than he was. Everything about the trip was all matter-of-fact to them—JFK International, the cabbie, the Waldorf. Although Adam was probably better traveled than most people his age, gliding through the busy streets of New York with the Thurmans made him feel that he had never been anywhere. He tried not to appear conspicuous as he peered out the window, awed by the scale and grandeur of the city with its row after row of skyscrapers, glittering storefronts, restaurants, and landmark hotels. Smartly dressed people walked briskly along the sidewalks with determined steps, all seeming to have somewhere important to go.

The cab stopped in front of the grand hotel, with its many flags wafting from the drafts that emerged from the enormous, tunnel-like spaces between the rows of skyscrapers across the city. Several bellmen approached the cab and seemed surprised by the few pieces of luggage for five people.

"We can carry these," Kellum instructed a bellman, giving him a five-dollar tip just the same.

"Y'all don't need to check in," Tilda instructed. "I got us a suite."

"Wow," Adam said, then felt awkwardly unsophisticated for having said it.

"Oh, it's great," Tilda said, which was her charming way of saying that the suite was worth a *wow* or two. Her tactful rejoinder made Adam feel less shy about gawking as they walked through the lobby of the Waldorf—which was, without question, the grandest hotel he had ever seen.

"What I love about this hotel is the rooms," Tilda said. "They're huge! I was just gonna get two adjoining rooms, but when I told Momma you were coming, Adam, she insisted that we get a suite so we'd be more comfortable. If I didn't know better, Adam Proffit, I'd say our momma has a big, fat crush on you."

Adam smiled bashfully.

"Tilda, stop, really. You'll make him tinkle," Kellum interjected.

"Too late," Adam chimed in, prompting laughter from everyone.

When they arrived at the door, Tilda handed the key card to Kellum, who opened the door so that Tilda, Mary Tate, and Su Su could go in first.

"After you," Adam said to Kellum.

"Nah, you go on ahead."

The suite was more opulent than Adam had imagined. After entering a small marble foyer, he stepped into a beautifully decorated living room with shantung silk curtains, antique French tables, and overstuffed sofas and club chairs covered in pale yellow linen. Doors leading to the bedrooms were on each side of the living room, and there was even an elegant powder room in case visitors came.

Adam had never seen a hotel room so beautiful. It was even prettier and far more lavish than the living room of his stepmother and father's house in English Turn, which, despite the great expense that had gone into its decoration, lacked the refinement, superb quality, and tasteful sophistication of the suite. He imagined the people who might have stayed here, perhaps presidents and diplomats, dignitaries and filmmakers. Yet the suite's genteel beauty seemed unremarkable to the Thurmans, and Adam suddenly felt embarrassed at how easily impressed he was by the room in which he was standing.

"That's your room," Tilda said, pointing to the bedroom on the right that had a king-size bed in the center. "Since there's three of us, we took the room with the two queens. But at least it's not a bunk bed like at Melbourne. Will you survive?"

"It'll be fine," Kellum replied, grabbing Adam's carry-on bag and tossing it along with his weekender bag onto the foot of the bed. "So, what's on the agenda?" he asked as he walked back into the living room and straight to the honor bar with a familiarity that suggested he had been there many times before. "Who wants a drink?" he asked.

"Oh, fix me a vodka tonic—you know, just the way I like it, with lots of lime," Tilda answered.

"Bourbon and water for me," Su Su said.

"Gin and tonic, love," Mary Tate added.

Kellum fixed the girls' drinks, and after Adam helped him pass them around, Kellum handed him a beer and then opened another for himself. They sat down in the living room and kicked off their shoes.

"So, Kellum, where are you thinking of for school next year?" Mary Tate asked.

"Not really sure yet. I was thinking of Vassar."

The three girls laughed.

"And how about you, Adam?" Mary Tate continued with a smile.

"Oh, I don't know yet. I'm going to throw a bunch of applications out there and see what sticks."

"He's being modest," Kellum interjected. "Mr. Proffit here has a four-point average and is probably going to be valedictorian. He doesn't have to throw his applications anywhere, 'cause the schools are all beating the doors down trying to get him."

"That's fantastic," Su Su said. "It's always nice to have smart friends. I'm still trying to find some." She took a sip of her bourbon as everyone else laughed at the smoothness of her delivery.

"Yeah, me too, Su Su sweetie, me too," Tilda said, holding up her glass.

*   *   *   *

After drinks, the four of them went to their rooms to freshen up for dinner.

"Man, those girls are a hoot, aren't they?" Kellum asked.

"Yeah, they're a blast."

"If I'm not mistaken, I'd say old Mary Tate has the hots for you. 'Course, she'll have to stand in line behind Tilda. You sure have a way with the ladies. I've never seen anything like it."

"Shit, Kellum, I've seen the way they all line up just to put their eyes on you at mixers. You're the ladies' man, not me."

"Yup," Kellum said, stretching his arms behind his head, "I guess you're right." He collapsed in the center of the bed.

Adam looked down at him, remembering all the tortured yearnings he'd had for Kellum before his more recent crush on Professor Moran. But with Melbourne so far out of sight, his old feelings for Kellum had begun to surface. The effects of alcohol and the sight of Kellum lying across the king-size bed seemed to be an invitation that would never arrive or for which there was simply no RSVP. Adam suddenly began to wish he had stayed at Melbourne. His frustration made him want to open the window and jump out, anything to end his pain and confusion.

"I'm going to take a shower," Adam said, his voice crackling faintly as he forced out the words as quickly as possible before he crumbled into pieces.

"You OK?" Kellum asked, looking up.

"Yeah, fine."

As Adam locked the door to the bathroom, he felt weak from the torrent of emotions that raged through him like a river that had suddenly changed its course. His body flooded with longing and sorrow that poured from a dark, secret place deep inside him—a place that had formed at the first vague instance when he began to realize he might be different from other boys—an imperceptible moment in time that began what seemed to be a life sentence of ridicule, pain and isolation.

Adam turned on the water spigot to the shower, flipped the switch for the ceiling vent, rotated the knobs of the sink, and looked around for anything else that might make noise. Then he collapsed to the floor and wept, wondering what was so wrong with him—why he had to fall in love with his best friend, a straight guy; why he had to fall in love with the unobtainable Professor Moran. Even surrounded by the people he cared for most, Adam felt lonelier than ever. He wanted to die.

CHAPTER 13

▼

BACK IN VIRGINIA

Carter closed the door to his apartment, relieved not to have to shake hands with any more parents. The day had been exhausting. It all seemed so effortless for the other faculty, who enjoyed hobnobbing with the social and political elite whose children attended Melbourne. But Carter was unused to such socializing, as it had never occurred within the shack of a house that had been his home for so many years in rural Mississippi. While he enjoyed the idea of meeting interesting people and loved films like *Gosford Park* in which socialites quipped, laughed, and glistened, Carter found that having to mingle with such people, as compared to watching them on the screen, was more tiring than he had ever realized.

*   *   *   *

"And this is Carter Moran, our newest professor," Jake Sommerville had said, introducing Carter to Winston and Weezie Harper, a stylish couple from New Orleans whose grandson was in the Third Form.

"Pleased to meet you," Carter said, shaking hands firmly with Winston Harper. Carter instinctively turned to offer his hand to Weezie Harper, who looked surprised, causing an awkward moment as Carter returned his hand to his side. A relieved, slightly amused look flitted across Weezie Harper's face, and she smiled at Carter.

"It's nice to meet you, Mr. Moran," said Weezie Harper. "I hope you won't take any offense, but I must say, if you looked any younger I would have thought you were one of the students."

Carter looked down at his feet bashfully as his face turned warm from blushing.

"Oh, I didn't mean to embarrass you," she continued, squeezing his arm gently as she flirtatiously inspected him from head to toe.

"Not at all, ma'am, I mean, Mrs. Harper," Carter fumbled.

"Now I do feel old," Weezie Harper exclaimed as she let go of Carter's arm and scowled slightly.

"Not to worry, son," Winston Harper said, patting Carter on the back. "We *are* old. No matter what my wife thinks. Anyway, it's good to see a few young faces on the faculty. No offense," Winston Harper said, turning to Jake Sommerville.

"None taken," Jake replied with a forced smile. "Guess I am getting a bit long in the tooth," he continued as Carter watched, slightly embarrassed at such a clumsy sycophant.

"Well, it probably would have been nice to have a few younger faces back when I was a student here," Winston Harper continued, this time patting Jake Sommerville on the back.

And so the reception had gone until Carter found the first opportunity to break away from the introductions and escaped out the back door of the building—discreetly leaving without saying good-bye, a tactic known among polite company as "taking French leave."

*   *   *   *

Back in his apartment, Carter collapsed onto the old but comfortable sofa and wondered whether his absence would be noticed at the later reception at Dunmore Hall, the headmaster's residence. However, he thought it would be better to miss the party than to go in a tired humor. Besides, as much as he enjoyed parts of teaching at Melbourne, he realized that it would never work out for him as a career. Conversations since he had arrived at the school had been peppered with enough off-handed, caustic remarks about gay marriage, the folly of a woman's right to choose, and urban underachievers to make clear to Carter that Melbourne would never accept an openly gay faculty member.

He realized now that he would have to remain in the closet, complete his year at the school, and leave Melbourne in good standing. He saw nothing good that could come of outing himself to the faculty. Telling the truth about himself, even in the unlikely event that he were allowed to stay, would certainly result in alienating him from the students who were the one part of Melbourne he really cared about.

As his thoughts turned to Adam Proffit, Carter felt certain that the handsome young Sixth Former had a crush on him. Carter realized the feelings were not one-sided but knew he would never allow anything to come of the attraction. He was convinced that during any future encounters with Adam Proffit, he would do everything possible not to send the wrong signals, the kind that might encourage Adam to believe that a relationship between them was possible.

The situation with Adam was awkward and uncomfortable, but Carter was most concerned about not doing anything to devastate the young man. He remembered how vulnerable he had been in high school, how easily shattered he would have been if he had acknowledged his sexuality to others the way that he was certain Adam Proffit was trying to acknowledge it to him. *What a great kid,* Carter thought. *He just needs to get through Melbourne and then maybe a few years of college, and he'll realize that there's a great big world out there, a world in which he can be whomever he chooses to be.* With only seven months before he would be moving to Cambridge to attend Harvard, Carter hoped he himself was also going to have opportunities to stop hiding his sexuality.

Carter had considered coming out to Adam privately, but sexual identity was such a delicate subject at Adam's age. Carter imagined that the first words out of Adam's mouth might be, "What are you telling me this for? I'm not gay."

Carter had read enough about gay people and their coming-out stories to know that no one feels at all comfortable disclosing their sexual orientation until they are actually ready, and the timing was different for each person. Until then, anyone raising the subject could be met with embarrassment and hostility. The range of unfortunate possibilities was limitless and even potentially fatal. *Best to leave it alone,* Carter thought. *Just try to be his friend without leading him on.*

There had to be other gay students at Melbourne, Carter knew. About four or five other boys, who appeared to be more conspicuously gay than Adam Proffit, came to mind. But those boys kept to themselves for the most part, and other students generally left them alone. Sometimes the boys whom he thought might be gay gave Carter knowing glances, but he always smiled back as if oblivious to the hidden message they were trying to send, which he imagined was, "I know." But, despite their self-imposed distance from the other students, at least the apparently gay boys seemed comfortable with themselves—or at least the ease with which they seemed to conduct themselves gave Carter that impression. Adam somehow appeared less comfortable with himself, unable to identify with the other possibly gay students who, at least to their credit, had all seemed to find one another. But then Carter wondered whether it would have been lonelier for Adam to identify with students who, despite their sexuality, might not have anything else in common. And then there was the stigma that any association with these students seemed to hold. And the attitude Carter sensed from these students caused him to think that if they knew about Adam, they would not be understanding of him but might actually use the information to hurt him for not openly joining their ranks sooner.

Stop it, Carter thought. *You're just projecting your own feelings onto this kid's.*

For a moment, Carter wondered whether he should discuss the situation with another faculty member, but he had yet to meet any to whom he could confide on such a matter. And speaking to anyone else raised the possibility of outing Adam, who seemed far too fragile to endure such an event without potentially dire consequences. Carter resolved that all he could do was to be the best faculty advisor possible—nothing more, nothing less.

CHAPTER 14

▼

PRINCESS DIPSY

Adam eventually emerged from the bathroom, shaven and showered, but his eyes were still slightly red from crying. He avoided looking at Kellum directly, hoping that he would not notice, hoping the traces of his distress would go away before anyone noticed.

"Hey, you OK?" Kellum asked.

"Oh, I'm fine," Adam responded, trying not to sound nasal.

"No, really, what is it?" Kellum repeated, standing up and taking Adam by the arms to prevent him from looking away.

"It's nothing. I got some shampoo in my eyes, and it burned like hell. I must be allergic to something in it. Weird, huh?"

"Do you want me to call downstairs and see if they have some eyedrops or something?"

"No, I rinsed 'em out pretty well. I think I'll be fine."

"OK, if you're sure."

Adam felt drained but had released his intense feelings, at least for the moment. He knew they would come back. They always did. He knew the entire cycle from beginning to end. It would begin with excitement at the prospect of finding someone to love, someone to love him. But the impossibility of it all, or perhaps just the improbability with the people he always found himself attracted to, would eventually land on him like a collapsed building. He would tear himself emotionally into a million pieces, certain that the pain was somehow his fault, that he was defective, perverted, and unworthy.

He thought about the people he had become attracted to. They were always, always unattainable. So many infatuations of his had never developed into anything. He had more hopes than realities, more desperate longings to find someone like himself for whom the attraction was mutual. He recalled the quarterback at his former school, whom Adam sometimes caught staring at him in class, but who barely spoke to Adam otherwise except to make a wisecrack to the other popular students about Adam's sexual preferences. Then there was his father's accountant, who had seemed amused, even pleased, by Adam's attentiveness whenever he visited the Proffits' house, but who never otherwise gave Adam an indication that his interest might be returned.

Adam felt certain he would go through life repeating the same venomous cycle, over and over, and would eventually die never having made peace with himself and never having found anyone to share the love he needed to share with someone special—like Kellum. *Oh, don't be so dramatic*, Adam would always tell himself after he had completed the cycle once more and as he tried to put the pieces of himself back together. His self-scolding was his signal that he still had hope, if not with the people he currently knew, then with someone somewhere in an undiscovered place that he hoped to find. This sense of hope would last for weeks, sometimes even months, until one day when he would wake up feeling desperately lonely all over again.

*   *   *   *

Adam sat on the bed and waited for Kellum to finish getting dressed. He was not yet ready to join the girls in the living room and wanted the redness in his eyes to dissipate a little more to avoid having to answer any questions about it.

"What do you think?" Kellum asked, holding up two ties next to his shirt.

"Definitely the yellow one," Adam responded.

Kellum threw the other tie back into his duffle bag and proceeded to fasten the one Adam had approved.

"You're gonna make someone a wonderful wife one day," Kellum chuckled as he continued fastening his tie.

"Whatever," Adam replied, resisting the urge to respond that if Kellum would only ask him, he would gladly take on such a role. Adam rolled his eyes exaggeratedly and tossed a pillow from the bed at his roommate, who ducked to escape the blow but muddled the knot he was tying in the process.

"Man, I'm gonna have to do it over," Kellum said with a grin.

"So, where are we going tonight?" Adam asked, changing the subject.

"We're gonna start at this dive called Princess Dipsy's, in the West Village. It's owned by this old black lady from Mississippi. They serve soul food and two kinds of wine, red and white, but I'd stick with the beer if I were you. After everyone's served, Princess Dipsy comes out of the kitchen, puts on some dazzle, and performs for all the guests. Boy, she can sure belt out the blues."

"Sounds amazing," Adam replied, perking up from Kellum's description.

"Oh, it gets better," Kellum continued. "The old broad gets more and more loaded as the night goes on. Then she gets kind of belligerent. Last time, she kicked everyone out while people were still ordering drinks, but I think that's part of her mystique."

"She sounds like a mess."

"Kind of. But I've had a few conversations with the old gal when she was still sober, and she's led a pretty amazing life. Her grandparents were slaves, so no telling how freaking old she is. She said she left Mississippi with nothing but a toothache. Now she owns her own place in the Village. It's kind of a dump, really, but in New York even a dump like that is bound to be worth about a million. I mean, I'm sure she bought it a long time ago, but she could probably sell the place and retire. Anyway, I think the old gal really loves what she does. Ya gotta admire that."

"Sounds great. How many times have you been?"

"Oh, 'bout three, I guess. You'll really like her. She's kicks."

✳   ✳   ✳   ✳

Princess Dipsy's was everything Kellum had described and then some. The building was old and dilapidated. Several rows of brick were losing mortar and sagging below the other rows, giving the side of the building a wavy appearance. As Kellum, Adam, and the girls walked inside, they could see that old metal colanders served as light fixtures and that the floor was covered in yellowed black-and-white linoleum, which had peeled up in several places. There were only about fifteen tables.

Kellum gave the hostess a tip, and she seated them at a good table at the front of the restaurant near the makeshift stage. The waiter arrived and collected the money for dinner, for which there was no menu. Apparently, Princess Dipsy had, in the past, kicked out so many patrons before they had paid their bills that prepaying had become a necessity.

The lights were dimmed, and the waiter placed two red votive candles at either end of the table. Then he brought out food on several large platters for each of the tables: red beans and rice, fried catfish, collard greens, fried okra, and spicy cornbread. Bottles of wine were delivered to other tables, while the waiter delivered an ice-cold pitcher of beer to theirs.

Adam and Kellum piled their plates high and ate seconds and then thirds, while Tilda, Mary Tate, and Su Su ate small portions.

"Go ahead and eat up, boys," laughed Tilda. "You're not gonna have food this good when you get back to Virginia. As for us, we're all watching our figures."

After the waiter had served lemon icebox pie, the lights dimmed further, and a black man in a dingy, red velvet dinner jacket stepped into the small stage area and ran his fingers across the keyboard of an upright piano. Then, in a raspy voice, he introduced Princess Dipsy, the Pride of the South.

Princess Dipsy stepped out of the kitchen wearing a full-length, white sequined gown trimmed in pink feathers that had worn away in various places, particularly under her arms. She was wearing a blond wig, à la Mae West, with feathers sticking out of one side.

The audience applauded as Princess Dipsy made her way to the mike. The piano player banged out a few chords before the Princess broke out into a loud, bluesy number echoing the story Kellum had told earlier about leaving Mississippi with nothing but a toothache, about the low-down dog who done her wrong, and, finally, about the victory dance she did when she arrived in the Big Apple.

By the fifth round of beers, Adam was well into a drunk, but the beers kept coming, and Princess Dipsy kept singing and drinking shots the waiter brought her between sets.

As everyone's eyes were on Princess Dipsy, Adam glanced over at Kellum, who was clapping along with the music, guzzling down beer after beer. He even looked good when he was drunk. After a moment, Kellum turned to Adam, realizing he was staring. He looked into Adam's eyes with a serious, sobering look, and then slapped Adam on the knee as he smiled widely, which both excited and saddened Adam at the same time.

Princess Dipsy was going at it hard when she swung her hand too far to the right and hit it against a tripod holding up a makeshift spotlight. She dropped the mike, which made a loud thud and a piercing echo. She lurched to grab the mike five seconds after it had already hit the floor.

"She's gawn freakin' pecawn," Kellum howled into Adam's ear, his lips touching his outer lobe and causing Adam's entire body to tingle, especially his groin.

It was the kind of thing that a straight guy would not have even noticed, but for a young man like Adam, it raised a million questions—or more like a myriad of hopes. Had Kellum's move been intentional, or unintentional, or even subliminal? Adam had barely begun to wonder about it when Princess Dipsy tripped over the tripod as she tried to recover her balance. Then she lurched into what seemed like a wild, flailing dance as her wig rolled off her head. She tripped again on an electric cord as she grabbed for her fallen wig and caught the hem of her dress under her right shoe. When Princess Dipsy stood up, holding the disheveled wig, the front of her dress suddenly ripped apart. In one swift second, all the commotion turned to complete silence as the packed restaurant of patrons stared motionlessly at Princess Dipsy, whose shriveled penis dangled pitifully between her legs amid the shreds of her evening gown.

"Aw, shit," Princess Dipsy said fiercely into the silent restaurant.

The quiet was suddenly broken by the infectious laughter of Tilda, whose arms were wrapped around her chest as if to prevent herself from splitting in two. "Oh, my God!" Tilda belted out, laughing. "She's a man! Whoo hooo!"

Tilda's vivacious cackling spread through the room like a highly contagious disease. Then the piano player started banging out another tune, and the other patrons began chattering loudly. Without missing a beat, Princess Dipsy took a bow and, in a slurred voice, thanked her guests and told them to have a good night. The crowd rose to a standing ovation as Princess Dipsy sauntered grandly out of the room, apparently undaunted as her penis still dangled between her legs.

*   *   *   *

They were still hooting from Princess Dipsy's surprising performance as they ambled back into the hotel suite.

"Nightcap, anyone?" Kellum bellowed.

The girls declined, followed by Adam.

"Good," Kellum said, "'cause I'm about to pass out."

With that, he strode into the bedroom and closed the door halfway.

"Good night, y'all," Adam said to the girls, who were disappearing into their room.

"Good night," they responded.

Adam stepped into the bedroom and closed the door behind him. Kellum had taken off his shirt and shoes and was clumsily trying to pull his trousers down as well. "Motherfucker," he said, fiddling with his belt buckle. Then his pants and boxer shorts both slid off, and he dove into the bed facedown, passed out. Adam stared at him intently. He was used to stealing glances at Kellum when he was naked, hoping not to be caught. Now he savored the opportunity to admire Kellum without fear of retribution.

Despite all the beer, Adam suddenly felt sober. He wondered whether to lock the door but then thought that, to the girls, that might seem stranger than if they found Kellum buck naked in bed. *Maybe I could just tell them I locked the door so as not to embarrass Kellum*, Adam thought, but then decided this sounded implausible. He considered sleeping on the sofa in the living room but quickly decided against it.

Adam turned off the light and undressed to his T-shirt and boxers, which he had to adjust because the sight of Kellum across the bed had excited him. Kellum's silhouette glowed from the streetlight seeping through the window. Adam sat up next to Kellum, who was taking up most of the bed, and caressed himself gently. Kellum did not move and began to snore softly. Adam slid across the bed and lay down next to him, with his face against the mattress. He stared at Kellum as he ground his hips slowly into the mattress, not wanting to rush but to savor the moment as long as possible. The certainty that Kellum was completely out made Adam feel braver. He lifted his hand and ran it gently down Kellum's back, then across his buttocks, which were firm and smooth. He gently massaged Kellum's crack, grinding the mattress harder. He pressed his hand against Kellum's body more forcefully, grinding the mattress with greater and greater force. It was all too exquisite to believe, at least until Kellum stirred as Adam's fingers reached down between his legs and touched the bottom of his scrotum.

"Huh," Kellum said, without even opening his eyes.

"Dude, you're taking up the whole damn bed," Adam said, having removed his hand, and then using both hands to shove Kellum to the other side of the bed, as if this had been his intention.

Kellum moved over and was quickly back to sleep. Adam was too terrified to risk waking him again and made love to the mattress as if it were Kellum.

*   *   *   *

The sun was beginning to rise above the Blue Ridge Mountains, and Carter emerged from the woods and made his way to the brick sidewalks that stretched from one end of the main campus to the other. He continued across the quad, a green lawn in front of the main row of original buildings dating from the early nineteenth century.

Carter had been unable to sleep and, after tossing and turning in bed, decided to take a walk that had led him from the formal environs of Melbourne into the vastness of the wooded hills surrounding the campus. Although it was unlikely that anyone else was awake so early in the morning, the campus somehow seemed even quieter with all the students away on Parents' Weekend. But then, the students were the raison d'être of the school, and it made sense to Carter that the place seemed empty and desolate without them.

He ambled along the sidewalk, admiring the Federal and early Greek Revival facades, when the name emblazoned across one of the buildings he had passed many times before caught his attention anew—Fitz-Waring Hall. It was an unusual name, one that Carter was certain he recognized, and suddenly he had an idea where he had seen the name before. He picked up his pace and walked excitedly toward the Monroe Building, darting up the various staircases until he reached C Dorm and the entrance to his apartment. The keys rattled as he fidgeted with the door, which he did not even bother closing behind himself. He scurried over to the box of personal books that he had brought to Melbourne, and which he had not yet bothered to unpack. One by one he pulled them out, tossing them onto the couch until he found the thin paperback he was looking for, *The Ties That Bind* by Elaine Fitz-Waring.

Carter flipped rapidly through the pages to the back of the book, where he scanned the author's biography. Elaine Fitz-Waring of Atlanta, Georgia, was the wife of Jack Fitz-Waring and the mother of two sons, Lawrence and Jack, Jr. Her book was the story of how the Fitz-Waring family had evolved when the older of the two sons revealed he was gay.

Carter set the book down on the coffee table and took from the nearby bookshelf the package of orientation materials about Melbourne that he had been given during his first week. He scanned each of the pages until he found the development package listing the names of all the major donors and the board of directors of the Melbourne School. He ran his finger down the alphabetical list to the F section, where he saw the name Jack Fitz-Waring, Atlanta, Georgia.

Carter's mind began to reel with excitement until it occurred to him that no one else on the Melbourne board of directors, faculty, or administration had probably ever read *The Ties That Bind*, a beautifully written but largely unrecognized account of how a prominent Georgia family had come to understand, accept, and become more tolerant after the elder son came out when he was in college. But despite the relative obscurity of the publication, Carter felt better about Melbourne, where, at least within the ranks of its esteemed board of directors, he suddenly felt he might have an ally.

CHAPTER 15

▼

NO GOING BACK

When Adam woke up, Kellum was still naked and sprawled across the bed. Adam slid out of the bed and stepped into the bathroom. He undressed and rolled his underclothes into a wad, which he would later stuff into the side pocket of his travel bag.

When he was finished shaving and showering, Kellum was still passed out on the bed. Adam dressed and walked into the living room to see whether the girls were awake yet, but they were not. He opened the door to the hallway and picked up the complimentary copy of the *New York Times* that had been left at the threshold. He read through it and did the crossword puzzle until the others started to awaken. He wanted desperately for Kellum to wake up, just to make certain he would act normally toward him, hoping that Kellum would not know, or at least not remember, what he had done. Adam scolded himself for having drunk so much and hoped that his drunken stupidity had not ruined the greatest friendship he had ever had.

All the girls had finished getting ready and ordered coffee and pastries from room service.

"Is my brother ever gonna get up?" Tilda finally asked, walking toward the bedroom where Kellum was still sleeping.

"Uh, Tilda, I wouldn't go in there. He's passed out buck naked on the bed."

"Nothing I haven't seen before," Tilda said. "Hey, girls, come get a load of my brother."

Su Su and Mary Tate scurried excitedly into the bedroom behind Tilda and jumped down on the bed beside Kellum, who did not even move.

"Wake up," Su Su said.

"Come on, Kellum, you lazy thing," Mary Tate added.

"Huh," Kellum finally roused. "What the fuck?"

"OK, girls," Tilda said, pulling the top sheet over her brother's naked body. "You've had your peep show. Now let him get ready so we can go hit the town." She turned back to Kellum. "Get outta bed, you sleepy head," she said, messing his hair before she led her two friends out of the room and closed the door. A few minutes later, she opened the door again and yelled, "Kellum, if you're not up and ready in fifteen minutes, I'm calling room service for ice buckets!"

This threat apparently did the trick, as Adam could hear Kellum moving from the bed as Tilda closed the door. It seemed like an eternity before Kellum finally emerged from the bedroom, clean and shaven, but with a hangover emblazoned across his eyes and face.

"Coffee, coffee, my kingdom for some coffee," he murmured as he dragged himself across the room and poured a cup of coffee, then plopped down close to Adam on the sofa and put his arm around him.

"Hey, buddy. You were pretty messed up last night. How are you doing this morning?"

If Kellum knows what I did, he certainly isn't showing it, Adam thought. For a moment, he hoped that Kellum did know and that he had enjoyed it. Deep inside, though, Adam knew this was not the case. Adam was grateful that Kellum had not woken up and thrown him out of the hotel room, telling him to fuck off and that he had better be out of their dorm room when he got back to Melbourne. But fortunately, the potential disaster had been averted by Kellum's apparent blackout.

The five of them spent the day wandering around New York. They first went to the Guggenheim and wandered through the original section and the new wing, admiring the artworks as much as the architectural marvel of the museum. Adam's eyes remained open wide, trying to take in as much as he could, feeling less uncomfortable about the obvious awe and excitement he was showing about everything he had seen.

"It's amazing, isn't it?" Kellum said, nudging Adam with his elbow as he walked beside him.

"What? The building, the paintings?" Adam asked.

"The whole thing. It's just amazing. I get blown away every time I come to this city. It's incredible, a remarkable place. I think I'd like to live here one day—maybe not forever, but I'd sure like to give it a shot. How about you?"

"I'm a little overwhelmed by it. There's so much, so many people, so many places to go. But, yeah, I think it would be amazing."

After the museum, they had Bloody Marys and then lunch at Tavern on the Green, which Tilda said was touristy but still a place everyone had to go on their first trip to New York. They went to Saks Fifth Avenue and Bergdorf Goodman, where the clothes and accessories were displayed with the same care and attention that the art works had been in the Guggenheim. Smartly dressed salespeople were in attendance and greeted customers with a casual nod and hello that implied they would remain unobtrusive unless needed.

When Adam thought no one might notice, he peeled back the label on a cashmere scarf and gulped awkwardly at the twelve-hundred-dollar price tag.

"Go ahead and say it," Kellum said, coming up from behind and smiling at him.

"What?" Adam asked, returning the scarf to its former position.

"Holy crap!" Kellum exclaimed with a smile. "That's what I said the first time I got a look at the price tags here."

"Huh," Adam replied, blood rushing up to his face as he blushed.

"It's OK," said Kellum. "This stuff is nice and all, but it's so overpriced. Mother and Tilda like to shop here, but me and Dad stick with Brooks Brothers."

"Yeah, I thought your clothes looked a little shabby," Adam replied jokingly. "You say that like it's Kmart or something."

"Nah, I didn't mean it that way. I mean…well, I don't know what I mean," Kellum replied awkwardly.

"It's OK, buddy. I'm just giving you a hard time," Adam replied with a smile that seemed to put Kellum at ease.

After shopping, they stopped for coffee from one of the dozens of Starbucks scattered across nearly every block in Manhattan. The hot café au lait traveled down Adam's throat, sending a wave of warmth through his body. It felt good to sit down for a while and even better to be squeezed up against Kellum as the Thurman entourage huddled around the tiny table at the coffee shop.

They finished the afternoon with a walk through Central Park, where the leaves were beginning to turn, signaling the advent of even colder weather. It was definitely the best trip Adam had ever taken, and he hated for it to end.

*   *   *   *

On the flight back to Washington, Kellum fell asleep, his head resting on a pillow that eventually slid against Adam's shoulder. Adam decided to allow himself, at least for the moment, to believe that the move had been intentional.

The flight attendant passed by and looked at Kellum nestled against Adam's shoulder. Adam smiled at her gently, hoping she was not offended at the sight of them. She smiled, then leaned over and turned off the light above their seats. She smiled at Adam again and then disappeared down the aisle.

Kellum stirred when the cabin shuddered slightly as the landing gear opened and descended for the final approach into Ronald Reagan International Airport. Adam peered intently out the window as the plane glided swiftly above the waves as if about to land in the Potomac.

"Man," Kellum said, straightening himself up in the seat and then stretching. "I was out."

"Yeah, you didn't move the whole way."

"So, did ya have a good time or what?"

"It was absolutely incredible. I can't even begin to thank you."

"Don't mention it. I'm just glad you had a good time, 'cause I had a blast. Man, when Princess Dipsy turned out to be a Prince—or Queen Dipsy—I thought I was gonna explode. Then old Tilda busts a gut laughing. I thought I was going to piss my pants."

"I know. I wasn't expecting that. Turns out a toothache wasn't the only thing Princess Dipsy left the South with, after all. She had her nuts too."

"Oh, man, that's raw."

They laughed loudly, and Adam felt overwhelmed with relief that his friendship with Kellum was still intact. He wanted to forget what had happened, wanted to forget the attraction for Kellum he had been harboring for so long and to enjoy being lucky enough to have such a good friend. *I wish I could be straight*, Adam thought, *because then I wouldn't have to feel this way. Then everything would be so easy.* Almost giddy with relief, Adam managed to push the emotions that so easily overwhelmed him back into the dark, empty place from which they had emerged.

CHAPTER 16

▼

BIG AGGIE

It was a clear spring day. The senior soccer teams were caked in dirt as they walked back to Dinwiddie Hall, the school gymnasium. Rain had been falling for several days, and the field was wet and slick with mud. There were no faculty coaches for senior soccer and very few rules, which made for rather aggressive playing. But after two students had broken their legs, the administration assigned two prefects to monitor the games and to help ensure that no one else was seriously injured.

Adam enjoyed senior soccer more than any of the other team sports he had played at Melbourne. It helped that he was good at it, but he also enjoyed having a break from the fiercely competitive organized sports. Soccer at Melbourne was good, clean, and, sometimes, rough fun.

"Man, I'm whipped," Kellum said as he and Adam walked up the steep hill to Dinwiddie Hall.

"Yeah, good game, huh," Adam replied.

"Hey, nice play, Proffit," Lucien Davenport said, panting as he caught up to walk with them.

"Thanks," Adam replied. He did not know Lucien well, although they had both been at Melbourne since their Third Form year. Lucien was one of the several students at Melbourne who tended to be loners and who only occasionally, but usually inappropriately, injected himself into other people's conversations.

Only a handful of students had private dorm rooms, which had to be specially requested, and Lucien Davenport was one of them.

It was hard for Adam not to feel sorry for him, but he usually overcame his tendency to pity Lucien by acknowledging the annoyance Lucien caused after only a few minutes in his company. Lucien had a few friends, but none of them seemed particularly close. They were mostly other students like Lucien who had not gravitated toward any group in particular.

Despite the small size of the student body, most of the friendships that people made during their first and second years laid the groundwork for the friends they would keep during the remainder of their time at Melbourne and, in many cases, for the rest of their lives. This fact accounted for the somewhat loose rivalries between dormitories, each of which was typically dominated by smaller groups of students who had selected their living arrangements based upon who their friends were. Adam and Kellum had both lived in the Monroe Building all four years at Melbourne. While the building had fewer amenities than many of the more modern dormitories, it was centrally located and housed the main dining hall, the commissary, the Rapp, and the bulletin boards where all the written announcements were posted. The Monroe Building was considered the main artery of the school.

"So, I heard you guys went to New York last weekend?" Lucien asked them now.

"Yeah, so?" Kellum replied.

"I don't know. How was it?" Lucien probed further.

"It was New York," Kellum said. "It was awesome."

"Did you get any poontang?" Lucien asked.

"Not that it's any of your business—and, incidentally, nobody says *poontang* anymore. Try *pussy* or *trim* or *snatch* or something else, but not *poontang*. But having never gotten any, you wouldn't know," Kellum said, smiling.

"So did you?" Lucien reiterated, undaunted by the remark.

"I don't know. Did I get any?" Kellum asked Adam, still smiling as if he knew what the answer was.

Blood surged from Adam's toes to his head, causing him to feel slightly dizzy and weak. He wondered whether Kellum had known all along what he had done in their hotel room and was now using the opportunity to toy with him. But Adam was certain Kellum was not that cruel and that he would not have waited until this moment, around someone with whom they did not socialize, to disclose Adam's sexual behavior.

"Yeah, Lucien. He had great sex. The best ever. I did too. You satisfied?"

"No, tell me the details?" Lucien asked, oblivious to the hint.

"Fuck off, you pervert. Go buy a *Penthouse Forum*. I'm not telling you about my sex life so you can go jack off about it in your room," Kellum added.

With this, Kellum high-fived Adam, who felt relieved that the exchange had ended.

They walked back to the locker rooms, undressed, and hit the showers, dumping their mud-soaked clothes into the giant cotton laundry baskets, from which they would be laundered and then recirculated the next day. There was no privacy in the shower rooms of Dinwiddie Hall. The walls and floors were covered in dull green tile, with a giant drain in the center of the floor that serviced the twenty spigots divided into two rows, one on either side.

As Adam watched the mud rinse away from his body, he thought about New York. He wondered about what Kellum had said, wondered whether he might know, or whether anyone else knew. Kellum had certainly not acted any differently toward him, and it seemed to Adam that they were even closer since their New York trip. His thoughts returned to their hotel room, to the sight of Kellum lying across the bed, Adam closing the door and turning off the lights, and then exploring Kellum gently with his hands.

"Goddamn, Proffit. You're getting a hard-on," Lucien said loudly, pointing at Adam's crotch and directing the other students in the shower to take notice.

Adam turned bright red and then retorted, "Yeah, well, I started thinking about how fine your mamma's pussy was when I fucked her last night."

This caused wails of laughter from the other students.

"You couldn't have fucked my mother last night," Lucien said.

"Why, were *you* fucking her again?"

More laughter followed.

Lucien puffed out his feeble chest and approached Adam as if taunting him to fight. His milky, pale skin was red with anger and clashed against his bright orange hair. "You're a big prick, Proffit, you know that?" Lucien said.

"Yeah, well, at least that's what your mamma tells me," Adam responded, laughing.

Lucien moved closer to Adam as if to take the altercation to the next level when Kellum stepped in between them and told Lucien to break it up unless he wanted to spend the next four weeks in demerit hall.

"Next time, Proffit. Next time."

"Yeah, bring it on," Adam said. "Bring it on."

*   *   *   *

Adam was reading through his mail when Kellum walked into their dorm room after finishing his morning classes.

"Get anything good? Any early acceptances?" Kellum asked.

"Nah, just a bunch of dumb catalogs and a postcard from Dad's wife."

"What are they up to these days?"

"Scuba diving in Belize."

"Sounds nice. We should go do that sometime," Kellum responded.

"That'd be great."

Adam's mother had died from breast cancer when he was five. While his father had always been something of a workaholic, he became more so after the death of Adam's mother. Adam had no brothers or sisters and had spent much of his childhood alone. He had faint memories of vacations taken while the family was still intact, but after his mother died, there were no other vacation trips. While Adam sometimes resented his father for not spending more time with him, the independence he had gained at Melbourne had transformed his sadness on the subject into a dull apathy. On some occasions, the weight of his existence made Adam too despondent to get out of bed. Kellum would try to cheer him up but quickly realized that Adam was better off left alone after he had fallen into the abyss of his emotions.

"Hey, want to get a shake at the Rapp?" Kellum asked. "I'm buying."

"No, thanks. I'm not really hungry."

"Come on," Kellum said, jumping onto the bed next to Adam and tussling him slightly. "You never have to be hungry for one of Big Aggie's shakes. They're sooooo good."

Adam smiled. He really did not feel like a shake but decided to go anyway. One of his dour moods was coming on, and he thought the change of scenery might help him to shake it off.

Kellum and Adam stepped to the end of the small line at the counter of the Rapp. Big Aggie, as she liked to be known, was behind the cash register while two other ladies of similar girth worked in the back preparing the food. Big Aggie was about five and a half feet tall and seemed just as wide, but she was always friendly and cheerful and never seemed to let anything bother her, despite the condescending attitudes that some of the more pretentious students sometimes showed her.

"What ya having today, baby?" Big Aggie asked when they reached the front of the line.

"Two shakes, Big Aggie, chocolate with whipped cream."

"What's the occasion?" Big Aggie asked.

"Haven't you heard? Old Adam here is gonna be valedictorian."

"Oh, my goodness," Big Aggie said. "I didn't know that. And that's worth celebrating. So just for today, your shakes are on me."

"Aw, thanks, Big Aggie."

"Don't mention it, baby. They'll be right out."

Kellum put a five-dollar bill in the tip bucket and then led the way to the booth where he always liked to sit. It overlooked the courtyard formed by the two giant wings flanking the Monroe Building, where students enjoyed hanging out between classes and, in some cases, smoking if they had been given written permission by their parents. About ten students had such permission and were habitués of the lush, green courtyard.

Other students who had picked up the smoking habit found hidden spaces around the campus where they could smoke without getting caught. These places included the steep roofs between the wings of the Monroe Building, onto which students could climb from the windows of the fourth floor—a place reserved by unwritten rule for Sixth Form students to take in the sun, hang out, and even smoke if they were so inclined. Smoking cigarettes without permission was not considered an honor violation but only a violation of the disciplinary code, and it resulted in ten demerits, the equivalent of two Saturday nights in demerit hall. A few students were widely suspected of smoking marijuana and, if caught, would have been expelled, but they were generally smart enough to be extremely discreet, choosing locations that likely included any of the remote corners of the sprawling fifteen-hundred-acre campus.

Big Aggie waddled over to the table, almost out of breath, and brought the two shakes, along with a small pitcher of the extra shake.

"Thanks, Big Aggie, but I'd have come and gotten them," said Adam.

"Oh, Lord," Big Aggie said, exhausted from having walked fifteen feet from the counter to their booth. "I need the exercise."

"Thanks, anyway," Adam said before she waddled back to the counter.

"You know," Kellum began in an uncustomarily sheepish tone, "I was thinking. What if we both get into Harvard or Yale or Princeton? What do ya say, roomie, would ya still want to be my roommate?"

"Wow," was all Adam could think to say. While he had often thought about how much he would miss Kellum after leaving Melbourne, the thought that they might attend the same college, much less continue rooming together, had not occurred to him as a realistic option. Then Adam thought about going through another four years of hiding his secret, of repressing his feelings for his roommate, and wondered whether he could endure it. At some point he would have to tell Kellum, and if he did, it would have to be before he and Kellum made any firm plans to live together. But he knew he could never do this at Melbourne. *So when?* he thought.

"Wow?" Kellum said. "You're the freaking valedictorian, and the best you can come up with is wow? Man, I've been dumped before, but baby, this takes the cake," he said with a cheesy smile.

"It's not that. I'm just, um, speechless, flattered, floored."

"So, what ya say, then?"

"Of course. I mean, yes, but what are the chances?"

"Well, I figure we're both in pretty good shape to get into at least some of the same schools, and you're more particular than I am about where you go."

Then Adam thought about his father, who had made it clear that he wanted Adam to attend Duke and had said he would not pay for him to go anywhere else. His father's income was too high to allow Adam to qualify for financial aid. While Adam had not forgotten Kellum's offer to fund his college years, Adam knew that the offer was something he could never accept, and he now declined the opportunity to remind Kellum that the offer had even been made.

"Well, I say we double our efforts on the apps, target the schools we want most, and then go from there. It would be awesome, wouldn't it?" Kellum said.

"It'd be amazing," Adam replied, believing the obstacles were too great to allow Kellum's proposal to materialize but not wanting to burst whatever bubble had carried Kellum to this particular decision.

CHAPTER 17

▼

AND THE WALLS CAME
TUMBLING DOWN

Adam took his seat in Professor Moran's English class and listened intently as the lecture began. Watching Professor Moran move from one side of his desk to the other, Adam thought about how easily his emotions and desires controlled him. He thought about the hotel room in New York where he had caressed Kellum as he slept, which, had this been discovered, could have easily destroyed their friendship. He thought about how attracted he felt to Professor Moran and how, despite the taboo of a teacher-student relationship, Professor Moran was the more suitable object of his attraction because—or at least, Adam believed—Professor Moran was gay, and Kellum was unlikely to be. Adam's emotional tee-ter-tottering caused the thought of drinking cyanide to cross his mind. *Better to get rejected*, he thought, knowing exactly what he had to do.

*   *   *   *

Carter was ironing the shirts he had just washed when he heard a knock at the door. He turned the iron off and placed it on the ancient ironing board that had no doubt been left in the apartment by a former faculty member during the 1940s.

Carter opened the door to see Adam Proffit standing with a notebook and several loose papers in hand. His white linen shirt was at least three-quarters unbuttoned, and Carter could not help noticing his smooth, tan chest beneath. The shirt was sloppily tucked into a matching pair of shorts in typical Melbourne fashion. "So, Mr. Proffit, what can I do for you?"

"Well," Adam began, "I've been working on my term paper and wanted to see if I might be able to run a few thoughts by you, both on the content and the direction it's going, and also on the organization."

They were the same words Adam had spoken dozens of times during the fantasy he was now planning to act out for the first time.

"Uh, well, wouldn't it be better to come see me during office hours?"

"I'm sorry. I didn't mean to bother you. I can come by Monday. It's just that there are only so many weekends left before the paper is due, and I wanted to get ahead so I could put some time in on my college apps. But it can wait."

Adam hoped that he sounded sincere enough that he could overcome the professor's probable reluctance to letting a student into his apartment, and apparently his ploy worked.

"No, that's all right," Carter replied with a slight reluctance in his voice. "Come on in."

The apartment was configured differently than Adam had imagined, as he saw the minute he stepped from the narrow hallway into the living room, where he saw a television perched in the corner. In his fantasy, the TV had been in the bedroom, but he anticipated there were some things upon which he would have to improvise.

"Have a seat," Carter said, pointing into the living room to a dated brown and green tweed chair, which was next to a sofa of similar vintage, where Carter sat down.

Adam looked down at the dingy brown carpet and decided that a little coffee spill could not make it much worse.

"Hey, Professor Moran, got any coffee?" Adam asked.

"No, but I might have some juice or maybe Coca-Cola."

"Oh, a Coke would be great, thanks."

"Let me see what I've got," Carter said, and he went to the kitchen to look in the icebox, which was as antiquated as the ironing board. He returned with two cans of Coke and handed one to Adam, who ran his fingers across Carter's hand as the man handed him the drink.

"So, now, what kind of difficulty are you having?"

"I think I may be trying to address too many issues, and it's diluting the impact of my thesis. So, in a way, I guess it's more of a structural or organizational problem. But there are so many points I want to make, and when I try to put them all together, it just becomes an incoherent mess."

"Sounds like a problem of broadening or narrowing your thesis to either eliminate the things that are not important or tie in the things that are."

Carter led Adam through a rather rudimentary discussion of the analytical mechanics of his paper. Taking care not to be obvious, Adam gradually turned the conversation toward his favorite books and authors, and soon Carter was fully involved with him in a discussion of Eudora Welty. The professor seemed amazed that someone as young as Adam was so familiar with the southern writer, who Carter had mentioned to the class was, by far, one of his favorites.

The plan was going much better than Adam had hoped. He continued to take small sips of Coke, saving the rest so that he could accidentally douse himself with it as soon as Carter left the room. The opportunity finally arrived when the telephone rang, and Carter excused himself to take the call in the kitchen.

Adam stood up and paced the room, hoping to find some shred of evidence—a letter, a photograph, anything—that Carter was the person Adam believed he was. He tried to overhear the conversation from the other room, waiting for a "good-bye" or a "talk to you later," which would be Adam's cue. "OK then," Adam finally heard, followed by the sound of Carter's footfalls.

Adam darted across the room and almost tripped as he reached for the Coke can. He paused briefly, and then poured its contents onto his shirt and shorts. But much to his surprise, the linen fabric repelled most of the brown liquid, which rolled off and onto the carpet.

"Damn it!" Adam said loudly.

Carter darted into the room to see what Adam was talking about and found his student holding the can of Coke, with some of its contents spilled onto his clothing. For a moment, Carter looked surprised, but then he smiled as if he recognized a clichéd method of seduction.

"Oh, this is going to stain," Adam said. "Mind if I use your sink?" He hoped Carter would not know his real motive, but as the older man smiled, Adam's spirits sank. *Oh, God*, he thought, *I'm sunk.*

"It's all right," Carter said, still smiling. "I'll get you a towel."

He disappeared into the kitchen, grabbed two clean wash towels, and ran them under the faucet. Then he returned to the living room, where Adam had already taken off his shirt. To Adam's delight, Carter began staring at Adam's athletic body, and a red flush began creeping up Adam's neck and onto his cheeks. As Adam stared back, Carter quickly averted his eyes, handed Adam one of the towels, and began dabbing with the other towel at the damp areas on the brown carpet.

Adam mopped hastily at the wet places on his shirt and shorts. "I think it's gonna stain, sir."

"Well, this should help. But if it stains, a little bleach will take it right out. I promise."

This comment was not in the script, and Adam suddenly wished he had opted for off-white clothes or some other color to which bleach could not be applied. He stopped wiping his clothing and sat down again on the tweed chair. He felt completely dejected, and his shoulders sagged. He couldn't help blinking rapidly to hold back tears as he began picking up his papers and preparing to leave.

Carter stepped closer to his chair. "Adam," he said, placing his hand on the boy's bare shoulder. Adam guessed that his teacher pitied him for his clumsiness and was trying to make a friendly, comforting gesture. Adam felt even more like a failure, a loser who would never be able to reveal his true feelings. His papers in hand, he stood awkwardly and prepared to leave.

Carter moved back a few steps. "Please sit down, Adam," he said. "Please."

Adam sat down, uncertain what to expect.

His teacher leaned forward, concern on his face. "Is there something you want to tell me? Something you want to talk about?"

"What do you mean?" Adam asked, defensively. "I'm just worried about the stains." He now wanted to escape, and he could hardly keep the tears from rolling down his cheeks.

"Adam," Carter continued, "I know you're different from the other students."

"Different? What do you mean?"

"I think you know what I mean, but it's up to you to determine whether, when, how, and with whom you share it. I'm not here to put you on the spot or to make you say or think anything you don't want to. But just answer one question for me. Just a yes or no question, with no hows or whys, ands, or buts—just without any explanation at all. Can you do that for me?"

"Uh, I guess." Hope flared in Adam's heart, and he let the papers fall into his lap.

"Adam, do you feel that you're different from the other students?"

Adam paused, then softly, still crestfallen, replied, "Maybe a little." The spark of hope grew, yet he was afraid to dare believe that Carter was really asking what he seemed to be asking. The beginnings of joy collided with the awful uncertainty, and to his own amazement and horror, Adam began crying uncontrollably, shaking, tears pouring down his face as he muttered and then repeated in a soft voice, "Yes, I'm different. I'm different. I know I'm different."

He felt Carter move next to him, crowding into the tweed chair with him, and felt the strength and warmth of his arms holding him tightly as Adam continued to weep until his cries faded into whispers.

When Adam was totally silent at last, Carter gave his shoulders one more squeeze and then broke away.

"Wait here," Carter said, and he soon returned with a few warm washcloths, which he used to wipe Adam's face, gently removing the tears and mucus. "Blow your nose into this," he said, holding a handkerchief to Adam's nose the way a parent does with a small child.

As Carter ran the washcloth over Adam's cheek, Adam pressed his face against Carter's hand and tried to kiss it. He was sure Carter had seen and felt the gesture, yet he did not respond, and Adam's humiliation caused him to break down all over again. Once more, Carter held him until he calmed down, and then wiped his face again.

"Professor," Adam said gently, in a broken voice, "I think I love you."

Carter leaned away and looked into Adam's eyes, which were bloodshot with loneliness, inconsolable pain, and disappointment. "It's OK," Carter said. "It's OK. You're going to be fine."

"But I think I love you," Adam repeated softly, leaning closer into his teacher's arms.

"Adam," Carter said quietly, "I'm sure you think you love me. But what you don't realize is that you barely know me at all. What you're in love with is the idea of love—and, believe me, it will come to you eventually. You just have to be patient. You're an absolutely incredible young man. And I promise, the day will come when you'll find someone as wonderful and deserving as you are. You're one of the brightest, most amazing kids I've ever met. Love will find you. You just have to be patient."

"I'm not a kid," Adam replied. "I'm almost eighteen. And you can't be much older than that."

"I'm twenty-two, but more important, I'm your teacher and advisor."

"That doesn't matter, 'cause I love you," Adam pleaded gently, beginning to break down again, both liberated and terrified at the same time, as if standing up to a menacing challenge that he had always feared.

Carter pulled him closer and held him intently, patiently, until Adam stopped trembling. Then he loosened his hold.

"People who are different, Adam—people like you and me—all feel that way at your age," he said patiently. "I know it seems like you're the only person on the entire planet who feels the way you do, but it's just not true. There are only a few hundred students at this school. But the world is a much bigger place, and it's filled with all kinds of wonderful, interesting, and different people. You just have to give yourself time and a chance. Can you promise me that? That you'll give yourself a chance?"

"I guess," Adam replied, his heart sinking. "I'm just so lonely." He felt on the verge of breaking down again.

"I know," his teacher said. "I know."

Carter took Adam into his arms to comfort him one last time. Adam clung to him and wrapped himself around him tightly. As he pressed his body closer to his teacher, Adam could feel himself becoming strongly aroused, and with a surge of joy he realized that he could feel his teacher's arousal as well. He prayed that somehow, some way, Carter would feel the same emotions that were overwhelming him. Adam needed that calm voice to turn savage with passion, and he tightened his hold, turning his face to find his teacher's lips.

At last their lips met, and to Adam's delight, his teacher suddenly melted against him, gliding his fingers across Adam's bare skin, creating an electrical response that made Adam's entire body tingle with excitement. Their lips met again and again, and their tongues explored each other's mouths. Their hands sailed the uncharted territory of each other's bodies. Exultant, Adam smiled widely. His stupid plan had achieved a far more beautiful result than he could possibly have fantasized.

Daringly, Adam murmured his teacher's name—"Carter"—and then pulled his teacher's shirt over his head. Their lips locked again. Adam's hands slid down the thick, coarse hairs of Carter's chest, then meandered to his shorts. He caressed Carter's erection, which was bursting through the material of his shorts, then slid his fingers under the waistband where his fingertips touched the tip of Carter's cock. Carter moaned.

They shed their clothes as if discarding cocoons in which they had been hiding their whole lives. They pressed against each other firmly, desperately, their tongues intertwined, their bodies tangled within the elegant pose of rapturous lovemaking. Their bodies compressed tightly, moaning softly, passionately. Then, in a single movement, Adam's muscles contracted uniformly as he leaned back and shot a long white stream onto Carter's chest. Adam reached down and began caressing Carter gently, up and down, rhythmically, their mouths locked, the vibrato of their tongues in unison with the movements of Adam's hands, until Carter tensed and hot liquid shot onto Adam's stomach in three discrete blasts.

Adam collapsed onto Carter, further mingling their thick, warm fluid, each drunk with exhilaration, two lifetimes of desperate longing and loneliness evaporating into the far reaches of the exosphere.

Carter awoke gently. Adam was still lying on top of him. *What the hell have I done?* he thought. *How did I let this happen?* He looked down at Adam's hair, with its golden brown streaks. He combed his fingers through it. Adam nuzzled up to him more closely.

"Adam," Carter said gently.

"Yeah," Adam looked up, smiling, then leaned in to kiss Carter, who turned his head away.

"Adam. This should not have happened. This never should have happened."

"But it did happen," Adam replied. "And it was incredible. The most amazing thing that's ever happened to me, ever."

"Adam, I'm your teacher. This is Melbourne. This never, ever should have happened."

"But it did, and I couldn't be happier," Adam said, holding Carter tightly.

"Adam, I've never done this before, with anyone. And I should not have allowed this to happen with you. I'm very, very sorry. It's my fault. It's all my fault."

"I seem to recall there are two of us," Adam replied, almost sarcastically. "And I'm not sorry at all. For the first time in my life, I feel like a whole person."

"That's what I mean. Adam, this is a very emotional thing. And, well, I just don't want you to get hurt. I'm your teacher. I'm your faculty advisor, for God's sake. I'm supposed to know better. I'm supposed to *be* better. You're not even eighteen, and I'm twenty-two." Carter wanted to hold tightly to Adam and never let go. His words were exactly what he thought he had to say, and exactly the opposite of everything that he felt.

"You're only four years older than I am. That's less difference than my dad and stepmom," Adam replied.

"It's not the same. I'm your teacher."

"You keep saying that, like it's supposed to mean something. I don't care. I've never met anyone like you, never had as much in common with anyone."

"Adam, it's not right. It's probably illegal. Oh, God," Carter said nervously.

"Hey," Adam replied. "Nothing was illegal. I'm of legal age of consent. Besides, I'm not going to tell anyone."

"Adam, you're going to have to leave. I mean, I'm not kicking you out, but this just can't happen. This shouldn't have happened. But I want to make sure you're OK. Are you OK?"

"Are you kidding? I'm fantastic. It's like, all my life I've felt like some kind of freak. Like there was something wrong with me. But when you were holding me, when we were—ya know—I've never felt more normal, more natural, more alive."

"Adam, this can never happen again. You know that, right? This can never happen again." Carter's voice was trembling.

"Why not?"

"Because it's not right. Not because it's wrong for two people, people like you and me, to have this happen, but because I'm your teacher. I'm not supposed to allow this kind of thing to happen. I can't believe I let it happen," Carter repeated, leaning down, rubbing his face with his hands.

"Hey, I wasn't exactly innocent in this. I mean, when I came here today, I wanted this to happen. I was dying for this to happen. The fact that it did seems like a miracle."

"Adam, you're great. I mean, you're amazing, and if we had met a year from now, when you were in college and I was in grad school, it might have been different. But this is now, and it shouldn't have happened."

"You keep saying that like it was something horrible. All my life I've felt so guilty about having these feelings, and then this amazing, incredibly beautiful thing happens, and you're making me feel dirty, disgusting all over again," Adam said, his eyes filling with tears.

"That's not it at all, Adam," Carter pleaded gently, taking Adam into his arms again, then pushing him away, finally holding him more tightly. "Please don't cry. We'll figure this out. And I did not mean to make you feel dirty. I'm sorry. I didn't mean to. The last thing I'd want to do is hurt you. That's the last thing I'd want."

Adam looked up into Carter's eyes and then put his head on his shoulder. They held each other tightly, afraid to let go, afraid of what waited beyond the door they had opened.

CHAPTER 18

▼

No One Will Know

"I've gotta go to the bathroom," Carter said, signaling that Adam would have to get up from where he was lying on top of him.

Adam slid to the side and could feel Carter's penis brush against his thigh as he slid across the man's body. Adam admired Carter's physique as he watched him walk out the room. Adam laid his head down on the sofa and looked up at the ceiling. He smiled contentedly. He felt lighter than he had ever felt before.

When Carter returned from the bathroom, he was wearing a pair of gym shorts. He sat down next to Adam, who felt the soft cotton material against his side. Adam suddenly missed the intimacy of their bare skin against each other. He turned to his side and pulled Carter into him, but he could feel Carter resisting.

"Adam, I'm very worried. I'm worried about you. I don't care what happens to me. But I don't want anything to happen to you."

Adam pulled Carter toward him, until they were lying next to each other, and looked into his eyes. "Nothing is going to happen. And I'm fine. I've never felt happier or more complete in my whole life. It's like, for the first time ever I feel safe and confident, like I could accomplish anything if I put myself into it."

"I'm glad to hear that. But I'm worried about the effects this could have on you. This isn't exactly the ideal situation for having your first…gay experience."

It felt as awkward for Carter to say the words as it felt for Adam to hear them. *Gay experience.* It sounded so clinical and cold, and too succinct to define the exquisite emotions he was feeling or the person into whom he had been trans-formed.

"You know," Adam said, brushing back a wisp of hair that had fallen across Carter's forehead, "all my life I've been trying to play by rules that, by their very definition, don't apply to me, don't include me. I was always twisting myself up, trying to live by other people's standards, until I thought I might snap in two. And this thing between us, whatever you want to call it, it's the first time I've been free from all those rules. Anyway, I know what you're thinking. It's written all over your face. You're worried because you're my teacher, and you're twenty-two, and I'm almost eighteen. But you know what? All those rules weren't made for people like us. And for the first time, I can see it all so clearly. And it's the most beautiful, most incredible thing."

Once again Carter found himself astounded by Adam's wisdom and maturity. Carter wanted so badly to believe that everything Adam had said was true, that the rules were not written for them—rules that made the task of seeking out oth-ers so formidable, stacking the odds against them, destroying the remote possibil-ity of finding someone to love.

"How did you get so smart for someone your age?" Carter asked.

"I have a great teacher," Adam replied, squeezing Carter tightly, wanting to hold onto him forever.

Carter thought about the fables his mother had told him as a young boy. The wily, thoughtful pelican had always known what to do. But of all the stories his mother had recited to him, none were appropriate to the situation in which he found himself. Of all the dangerous encounters the pelican had faced, he had never had to confront himself. Or perhaps that had been the point all along—that the pelican had always been true to himself, and that, above all things, had allowed him to survive.

*   *   *   *

They lay close together for several more hours, which seemed like minutes.

"It's going to be lights-out soon," Carter said. "You'll have to leave."

"I know," Adam sighed, holding Carter tightly. "But I don't want to."

"I know too, but there are some rules we have to follow."

"I guess you're right," Adam replied, then leaned into Carter and pressed his lips against his. At Adam's touch, Carter's mouth opened, and the electricity began anew. Carter could feel Adam becoming aroused, and Adam began to grind himself against him. Adam reached down into Carter's gym shorts and began stroking him gently. Adam pulled Carter's shorts down until he caught them with his foot, which he used to push them off the rest of the way.

Adam ran his lips down Carter's chest to the bushy patch of pubic hair, which smelled like concentrated Carter—a combination of musk and spice, like the smell of an unlit pipe. Adam kissed the top of Carter's penis, then gently took it into his mouth, caressing it with his tongue, massaging it with his lips, delicately running his fingers across Carter's balls, and gently stroking the bottom of his penis with his other hand, the way he had imagined doing so many times before.

Carter's entire body contracted with the smooth, rhythmic movements of Adam's hands and mouth, pulsing, caressing, aching, longing. Carter began to convulse, and Adam knew he was about to come. Adam removed his lips and stroked Carter's penis, squeezing gently, up and down, until shots of cum soared across Carter's chest. Adam stood on his knees and edged up the sofa until his hips were above Carter's face.

"My turn," Adam said, opening Carter's mouth with his fingers and sliding himself in, then pulling out, fucking Carter in the mouth. Carter mimicked the gentle hand gestures that Adam had used only moments before, but allowed his fingers to improvise. Adam slid in and out, pressing himself firmly into the roof of Carter's mouth, thrusting, convulsing, tingling—then, with one last surge, pulled out, grabbing himself tightly with one hand as he shot hot cum all over Carter's neck and chest. Adam collapsed onto Carter one more time, inhaling the organic smell of their sex.

"OK," Adam said, rising up a little. "Now I'm ready for lights-out."

$$* \qquad * \qquad * \qquad *$$

After they had showered, dried off, and dressed, Adam casually stepped out of Carter's apartment and into the hall. He saw no one as he stepped away from the apartment, but he wanted everything to look normal in case anyone happened to walk by. "Thanks, Professor Moran," he said with a wink.

"Uh, no problem," Carter replied awkwardly.

"See you in class tomorrow."

"OK, then," Carter said, then closed the door.

Adam felt light as air as he walked down the long flight of stairs and through the hall to the room he shared with Kellum.

"Hey, where ya been?" Kellum asked when Adam stepped into the room.

Kellum was lying across the top of his bed in boxer shorts and no shirt, reading a book. Kellum's appearance, hours earlier, might have driven Adam wild with lust. But now he could ignore it, and that made him feel good. Suddenly it did not matter whether Kellum did this kind of thing on purpose or whether he was oblivious to the way it made Adam feel. Either way, Kellum would always make himself off-limits, just as he had always done, and for the first time since they had been rooming together, Adam genuinely did not care.

"Oh, just wanted to get a little ahead on my term paper," Adam replied, suddenly realizing that he had left all of his papers in Carter's apartment.

"Oh, yeah? Well, where are your books?" Kellum asked, turning to his side.

"I left them in the library. I was going to get a Coke at the Rapp and then just didn't feel like going back. I'll grab 'em tomorrow on my way to class."

At any other school, Adam's lie might have seemed implausible. But with Melbourne's strictly enforced Honor Code, students could leave their personal belongings almost anywhere without having to worry about whether they would still be there later. While stealing was rampant at other boarding schools, taking as much as a pencil without the owner's permission was grounds for immediate expulsion from Melbourne. Lying was an equally punishable offense, Adam knew, but that lie was necessary and seemed to have gone undetected when Adam later retrieved his papers from his in-box in which Carter had promptly placed them early the next morning before it seemed anyone else was awake.

"You work too much," Kellum replied, turning his attention back to his book.

"What are you reading, anyway?"

"*Catcher in the Rye.*"

"Why? God, I haven't read that since Third Form," Adam remarked.

"Yeah, I just wanted to read it again. I'm not sure why. I guess I think about how fucked-up old Holden Caulfield is, and it makes me feel like less of a fuck-up myself."

"Less of a fuck-up? Have you looked in the mirror lately, Mr. Prefect, Mr. Varsity Lacrosse?"

"That's all appearance, Proffit, all appearance. On the inside, I'm a big jumble of mess, trying to grab for the brass ring like everyone else."

Despite the invitation to inquire further, Adam hesitated. For once he did not want to care about how Kellum thought or felt. He suddenly resented all of Kellum's innuendo and ostensible game-playing. Other than possibly being a little curious about his roommate's sexuality, Adam wondered what Kellum could possibly be upset about.

"I think the brass ring was laid at your feet a long time ago," Adam retorted. "You just never bothered to look down toward the rest of us to see it."

"Well, on that note," Kellum responded, his voice breaking slightly as he jumped out of bed and flipped off the lights.

It sounded like Kellum was about to cry and did not want Adam to notice. Adam thought about all the times he had silently cried himself to sleep thinking about Kellum. It was as if all the love, lust, and anguish he had felt about Kellum had turned suddenly into dislike and resentment.

You're too late. I've already found someone, and he loves me. I know he loves me, Adam thought as he drifted off to sleep.

CHAPTER 19

▼

REGARDING HOLDEN

"Get outta bed, sleepy head," Kellum said as he walked into the room wearing his towel, just back from the shower.

Adam stretched languorously, thinking about all that had happened the day before. He remembered Kellum and how uncharacteristically fragile he had seemed the night before, and how callous Adam had felt toward him. Adam marveled at how far the pendulum of his emotions had swung him into a place he had never been before.

"Hey, buddy, are you OK?" Adam asked.

"I'm great. What do ya mean?"

"Well, you seemed kind of upset last night, not yourself, ya know."

"Ah, I probably got a little too much into old Holden Caulfield's head, that's all. That book always works on me like that."

"You sure? I mean, you're OK?"

"I'm fine, Proffit. Now get outta bed and get ready, or I'm going to go on to breakfast without you."

He was back to being the old Kellum—or at least, the only Kellum anyone was allowed to see. Adam wondered whether underneath the golden-boy exterior Kellum was just as tortured and messed up as he himself had always been. Whether the pain was about his sexuality or about something else, Adam felt a knot in his stomach for not having been a better friend to his roommate on such a rare occasion when Kellum had revealed a bit of vulnerability. Adam wondered whether all the Thurmans put up as good a front as Kellum and whether deep inside they were all as fractured and confused as everyone else.

"You gonna get outta bed or what?" Kellum repeated, interrupting Adam's train of thought.

"Oh, yeah, just dozing off again. Sorry."

*   *   *   *

Adam stood under the shower, his thoughts turning from Kellum to Carter. He started becoming aroused and quickly tried to focus on something else, praying not to get a hard-on. He lifted his arms to rinse the soap from his armpits, then turned off the water and quickly fastened his towel around his waist. He was almost half-hard and could feel himself getting harder as the terry cloth chafed his penis. He knotted the towel in the front to try to conceal what was beginning to poke out underneath and wondered how he was going to get through a whole day of classes, much less the rest of the semester, if this was going to happen every time he thought about Carter.

"That was fast," Kellum said when Adam walked back into the room.

Adam stood with his back to Kellum as he unfastened his towel and pulled a pair of briefs and a T-shirt from his chest of drawers. He quickly pulled the briefs over himself and positioned his erection to the side, then pulled his T-shirt over his shoulders and down below his waist.

"Tighty whities? What's the occasion?" Kellum asked.

"And I was beginning to think you didn't care," Adam replied dryly, trying to avoid revealing the real reason, which was that he would have stuck out of boxer shorts like a rocket. "How do they make my ass look?" Adam asked, modeling his backside.

"Awesome. I can hardly control myself. Damn, you're hot. If I had less control, I'd have to fuck you right now."

"All you ever had to do was ask," Adam admitted, taking the banter to a level that he never would have been brave enough to attempt before. But he was tired of the games and dishonesty. If Kellum had those kinds of feelings for him, he would rather get them out in the open than waste any more time agonizing over how Kellum might actually feel.

"What, no candles, no champagne? You're a real romantic, Proffit."

"Well, just being honest." Adam replied without the usual tone of sarcasm.

"Come on. We'll be late for breakfast," Kellum said, standing up as Adam tucked his shirt into his shorts and slipped into a pair of flip-flops.

"I'm coming."

*   *   *   *

Carrying his breakfast tray, Adam followed Kellum to their usual table. Several of the other prefects were already there eating breakfast.

"You look like shit, Thurman. What the hell?" asked Mason Bird, who was known by the other prefects as Birdy.

"Just couldn't sleep last night."

"What? Did Proffit keep you up all night beating off again?"

Adam looked across the table at Kellum, wondering what he knew and whether he would have mentioned it to any of the other prefects. *But Kellum would never do that*, Adam thought—or at least, he hoped.

"No, I guess maybe I was just a little too loud when I was fucking your mother up her ass last night, Birdy. Sorry, Kellum, didn't mean to keep you awake," Adam quipped.

"No problem, buddy," Kellum added.

"I guess that's the way you like it, huh, Proffit, up the ass?" Birdy retorted.

"Yup, that's exactly how I like it," Adam replied, still riding the wave of honesty.

"Jeez, Proffit, keep it to yourself," one of the other prefects added. "I'm trying to eat my fucking breakfast over here."

"Sorry, just answering the question," Adam replied.

"Well, don't."

Just as this repartee concluded, Boris Yurgen, an exchange student from Germany, set his tray down at the table with Adam, Kellum, and the other prefects, causing several of the prefects to look askance at one another. While Boris tended to keep to himself most of the time and had not really made much of an effort to befriend anyone in particular at Melbourne, he occasionally made attempts to join the other students, apparently oblivious to Melbourne's unwritten social mores, which included not sitting at the prefect table unless invited. Boris's attempts often prompted sarcastic remarks directed at him, though he usually seemed not to understand them and responded with good humor.

"Hey, Boris, what are you gonna do this summer, work at Burger Führer?" Birdy asked, prompting waves of laughter from the table.

"Hah, hah, you amuse yourself so well," Boris replied in his thick German accent. "There is no such thing as a Burger Führer."

"That's right," Birdy said. "We did win the war."

"Yes," Boris replied. "You have made the world safe for your imperialist Burger King."

CHAPTER 20

▼

A SCHOOL NIGHT

Adam had felt apprehensive all morning in anticipation of English class, which would be the first time he would set eyes on Carter since their rendezvous the night before. As Adam filed into the room behind other students and took his assigned seat, he tried not to stare at Carter, who was sitting on the front of his desk as usual. Carter looked more handsome than usual, but his eyes seemed a little bloodshot and tired, as if he had not gotten enough sleep.

"OK, everyone, I'm passing around a pop quiz. You have twenty minutes for the questions, and you may hand them in at the end of class," Carter instructed as he handed the quizzes to a student in the front row, who proceeded to pass them around amid the low, dull moaning of the classroom. "I'll be back."

Carter stepped out of the room, and the students began reviewing the questions, some of which required short answers and some of which required analysis. Adam watched Carter's stride as he stepped out of the room, and they made eye contact briefly before the door closed. *He handled that pretty smoothly*, Adam thought.

Adam's mind wandered from the quiz questions to the events of the night before, and he could feel himself getting hard all over again. He looked down at the quiz and tried to concentrate on his answers. As he pondered the questions, he could feel the swelling in his shorts going down. Relieved, he concentrated even more. *This won't be so tough*, he thought.

But Adam found it much more difficult to concentrate after Carter stepped back into the classroom. He tried to remain focused on the discussion, but steamy images of his night with Carter kept running through his mind. When Carter turned to write on the chalkboard, Adam's eyes wandered along the contours of his muscular frame. He remembered Carter's fingers running down his back. *Stop it*, Adam thought, and he returned to the questions before him.

Adam's emotional teeter-totter continued until class let out. Adam lingered intentionally behind the other students as they ambled out of the classroom, placing their quizzes on Carter's desk as they left.

"Here, Professor," Adam said, handing his quiz to Carter.

"Thank you, Mr. Proffit," Carter said, taking the exam from him, smiling, very cool and controlled, not giving anything away.

"See you later," Adam said.

"OK, then."

*   *   *   *

It was Monday night. Adam lay down in his bed and waited to hear Kellum begin the steady breathing that would let Adam know he was asleep. This seemed to take longer than usual, although Adam was fairly certain he was just feeling anxious and impatient. He was getting hard just thinking about Carter, whom he had not seen since class that morning, and with whom he had not had a private moment since Saturday.

Kellum's light breathing finally came, signaling that he was asleep. Adam crept out of his bed. He grabbed his robe from the chair on which he had intentionally left it, and began to tiptoe out the room.

"Where ya going, Proffit?" Kellum asked in a sleepy voice.

"Just to the bathroom. Go back to sleep."

"All right."

Adam had already come up with a number of excuses, which included getting a glass of water, having a smoke, or, if it was a weekend, herding the cattle, which was a Melbourne custom known as *Saturday night ranch handling*. Melbourne had its own dairy cattle, and every once in a while, small groups of students, usually Fifth and Sixth Formers, would sneak out at night and into the pastures to rustle the cattle. Sometimes the cattle would not even move, but other times they would stampede wildly in the pitch-black night of the Virginia hills. The success of the outings was usually determined by how loud and boisterous the ranch handling became, which was directly proportional to how scary it was and the likelihood of getting caught or severely injured. Although no one had ever been expelled from Melbourne for ranch handling, getting caught could likely land a student in demerit hall for the rest of the year.

Adam crept down the hall and gently up the stairs to the landing of C Dorm, where Carter's apartment was located. He tapped gently at the door and listened for footsteps from within. When he did not hear any, he tapped again, a little harder this time, and waited. Still nothing. He could see a flashlight coming down the hall and quickly hid behind a nearby door that had been left standing open. No doubt the flashlight belonged to one of the faculty members making the evening rounds.

Adam stood motionless behind the door, trying not to breathe, as the flashlight approached, closer and closer. *Holy shit*, Adam thought. *How am I going to explain this? Holy shit, holy shit, holy shit.* The flashlight stopped when it reached the landing, and Adam stood still, hoping it would pass. Then he heard the switch of the flashlight and saw the light go out. *Motherfucker*, Adam thought, *I'm totally busted.* But then he heard the rattle of keys and the sound of a door being unlocked. It was Carter—or at least, Adam thought it was Carter. He waited until he heard the door close, and then he crept out, again tapping softly on Carter's door. This time he heard footsteps, and the door opened.

"Adam? What are you doing here?" Carter asked.

"Can I come in?"

"Well, uh, yes, come on in," Carter replied nervously, looking around to make certain that no one was about.

"I'm sorry. But I had to see you."

Carter closed the door and turned around. "Adam, this is very risky. It's a school night. Do you know how easy it would be for you to get caught? Now what good would that do?"

"I don't know. To be honest, I don't care. I just needed to see you."

Carter looked worried. It was not the expression Adam had been imagining. He had hoped Carter would take him into his arms, murmuring that he could not have stood another second without seeing him.

"This is just too risky," Carter said. "And besides, I've been doing a lot of thinking, a lot of thinking. Here, come in, sit down."

Adam followed Carter into his tiny living room and sat down next to the sofa where he and Carter had made love a few days earlier.

"Adam, I think you're amazing, and if you were a little older, if we weren't here—well, I'd be crazy not to be with you. But the fact of the matter is that we *are* here, and you *are* younger, and I am your teacher. As much as I would like to,

I can't go through with this. I never should have let it get as far as it did. I never should have let it get anywhere at all. Do you understand?"

"But," Adam began, his eyes filling with tears.

"Adam, please, look at me."

Adam looked up at Carter, who appeared to be in equal anguish.

"Adam, you were and always will be my first. I am so astounded by you. That's what made this happen in the first place. You are so damn amazing. But the risks are too high. More than anything, it's just not right for me to be with you now. As hard as I've tried, I just can't get past being your teacher. It's not about the age thing. It's about our roles. It's about my responsibility as your teacher and advisor. And it's my fault because I let my feelings for you cause me to cross a line that should never have been crossed. Do you understand?"

"I think so," Adam replied, dejectedly.

"It doesn't mean we can't be friends—good friends—and maybe one day, who knows? Maybe we can be more in the future, but now, we can't be anything more. That's all I can give you, and I hope you can accept that. Can you?"

"I guess. But what does this mean?"

"It means we can't see each other—not like this, not after hours, no slinking or sneaking around. You can come see me any time in my office, though. OK? It's the only way we can keep it safe. Do you understand?"

"Not really."

"Please try to understand, not for me, but for you. I'm doing this for you. You're too young, too vulnerable. Trust me. I know exactly what you're feeling. It's those feelings that led to what happened in the first place. Just promise me that if you ever need to talk, you'll come see me in my office. That'll be safer for both of us. You're incredible, Adam Proffit, and I know you can do this. You're much stronger than you think you are."

"But I'm not," Adam pleaded, and he threw his arms around Carter. "I'm not."

"Yes. Yes, you are," Carter repeated softly, stroking the back of Adam's head affectionately. "Yes, you are."

They held each other for several minutes, and then Carter pulled away. "Come on, let's wash your face and then get you off to bed."

Carter led Adam into the bathroom and ran a washcloth underneath the water, then wiped Adam's eyes, nose, and mouth. "See, good as new."

Carter led Adam back to the doorway. "Adam," he began, "whatever you're feeling, keep telling yourself that this is for the best. OK? Promise me that?"

"I'll try," Adam said, and then slipped out of the apartment, tiptoed down the stairs, and crept back to his dorm room.

"That must have been some crap," Kellum said as Adam threw his robe back onto the chair. "You sure were gone a long time. You OK?"

"Yeah, I'm OK. It was just the mother lode."

CHAPTER 21

▼

THE GESTAPO

"OK," Carter said, beginning the class, when the students' attention turned from Carter to a knock at the door.

"Uh, Professor Moran, Mr. Wirth needs to see you," said Mason Bird, one of the prefects.

"Right now? I'm starting my class."

"Yes, right now. Please go on ahead. I'll stay with the class."

"OK, then," Carter replied, wondering what could be so important.

Carter walked briskly out the humanities building and toward the Monroe Building, where the headmaster's office was located. When he arrived at the headmaster's office, Shasta Brockman was sitting behind her desk.

"Go right in, Mr. Moran," she said coldly, without any of the usual repartee that accompanied visits to the headmaster's office.

Carter stepped through the door and into the office, where Mr. Wirth was sitting behind his desk and Jake Sommerville was sitting in a nearby chair. Neither stood up to greet him.

"Please sit down," Mr. Wirth instructed.

"What can I do for you? What is this about?" Carter asked.

"Mr. Moran, it has come to our attention that one of our students was seen coming from your apartment rather late last night, after lights-out, when you were supposed to be on rounds. The student was not," Mr. Wirth paused, "fully dressed. Do you have an explanation for this, Mr. Moran?"

"Uh, well, yes," Carter replied nervously, tiny beads of sweat erupting from every pore. "Yes, Adam Proffit did come to see me last night. He was pretty upset—about his term paper, college admissions, that kind of thing. I knew it was late, but he seemed distraught. I figured that as his faculty advisor, I couldn't turn him away. I know I should have told him to come see me in the morning, but I worry about these kids, under so much pressure, and when someone comes to see me that late, it seems like a warning sign that I shouldn't ignore."

It was all a big lie, but once Carter started with his explanation, he found himself unable to stop, rambling on and on. All the while, he had the sensation of falling, even though he did not move, frozen in his seat, hoping they could not see the sweat erupting underneath his arms, dripping down the insides of his shirt, as the words continued to sputter from his mouth.

"I see," Mr. Wirth replied. "All right, that will be all, Mr. Moran. You may go back to your class now. I'll let you know if we need anything further."

"Thank you," Carter replied. He stood up and shook hands with Jake Sommerville and Mr. Wirth, and then left the office.

As he walked back to the humanities building, he wondered what would happen next. But he had learned enough during his orientation to gain an idea of how it would probably play out. Adam would be called into the headmaster's office and then, following his interrogation, could likely be called before the Prefect Board to determine whether an Honor Code violation had occurred. Depending on the decision they reached, both Carter and Adam could be asked to leave the school as early as that afternoon. Then an unscheduled assembly would be called after dinner, and Mr. Wirth would advise that one of the students as well as one of the faculty had been asked to leave the school, followed by a description of the circumstances leading up to the decision.

Carter wondered what words Mr. Wirth might choose to tell the students about what had happened. It could be as simple as telling them that a student had lied and a faculty member had tried to cover it up. No doubt Mr. Wirth would omit any suggestion of sexual impropriety, as this kind of thing simply never occurred at Melbourne.

A letter would follow to Harvard, advising that Carter had been terminated early for shortcomings of moral character or some other euphemism that would raise more questions than it would provide explanations about what had happened. Adam's father would not even pick him up from school. A taxi would arrive instead to take Adam to Reagan International Airport, where a plane would rush him home to his father and stepmother in Louisiana. His parents would probably then elect to send Adam to a military school that accepted students who had been kicked out of other schools. It would be a place ill-suited to someone of Adam's sensitive nature. He would start using drugs, probably pot at first, but then progress to cocaine, maybe even heroin, then end up on the streets, homeless, prostituting himself for a fix.

And it was all because Carter had lacked the emotional control to prevent anything from having happened between Adam and himself. Carter thought about jumping off the Rappahannock Bridge and drowning himself in the river, but he knew his death would do nothing to help Adam, who, at that moment, was his only concern.

CHAPTER 22

▼

THE INQUISITION

Adam was sitting in Chemistry 602 when a knock at the door interrupted his class. One of the prefects whispered to Professor McGill, one of the longtime teachers at Melbourne.

"Mr. Proffit, please excuse yourself from my class and accompany Mr. Bird here to see Mr. Wirth," Professor McGill instructed in his ratchety voice, which made him sound angry despite the fact that he was one of the most congenial professors on the faculty.

A murmur throughout the room made Adam's heart beat even faster than the prospect of being sent to Mr. Wirth's office. Calling out a student during the middle of class could mean only one thing—somebody was going before the Prefect Board, and whoever it was, Adam Proffit had something to do with it. Several of the students looked at each other with questioning looks, for which there was no affirmative answer.

"So, what's this about?" Adam asked Mason Bird as they walked down the hall of the science building.

"Proffit, you know I'm not allowed to discuss it. Just wait until you see Mr. Wirth."

Adam was startled by the formality with which Mason Bird addressed him. While they had not been close friends, they had always enjoyed a spirited banter, which this exchange lacked completely. They were silent for the remainder of the walk to the headmaster's office.

Adam thought about what the reason could be, wondering whether his relationship with Carter had something to do with it. But no one else knew, and Carter had certainly not told anyone.

"Thank you, Mr. Bird, that'll be all for now," Mrs. Brockman instructed as they arrived at Mr. Wirth's office. "You may wait in the Prefect Room until further notice."

Holy shit, Adam thought. *The Prefect Room? This is serious.*

He stepped into the paneled office of the headmaster, who was sitting behind his large desk with a menacing look on his face. Mr. Sommerville, the assistant headmaster, was standing by his side.

"Sit down, Mr. Proffit," the headmaster commanded.

"What is it, Mr. Wirth? Did I do something wrong?" Adam asked.

"Well, that remains to be seen," Mr. Wirth replied abruptly. "Tell me about your relationship with Professor Moran."

It was an open-ended question, but Adam assumed what he was getting at.

"Well, sir, he is my faculty advisor. He's been a really great friend to me this year. He's not that much older than I am, I guess, and I just feel that I can relate to him well, especially with all of the college admissions coming up."

The headmaster and Mr. Sommerville looked at each other, and Adam realized that although they seemed pleased with his answer, they would ask more pointed questions.

"Mr. Proffit, have you ever been to see Professor Moran after lights-out?"

Holy shit, Adam thought, hoping that they could not tell how nervous he was. *Motherfucker. What do I say? Simple*, Adam answered himself. *Keep it simple. Tell the truth—as much as possible.*

"Uh, yes, sir. Matter of fact, I went to see him last night." *That was good*, Adam thought. *Yeah, that works. They're buying it. God, please let me get through this. Please don't let me get kicked out. Please.*

"Why, Mr. Proffit? Why did you go see him last night?"

"Well, um, I couldn't really sleep." Adam paused, trying to figure out his next move. "I've been all stressed out about my term papers, about my college apps, getting financial aid wherever I go, about my GPA."

Adam watched nervously as Mr. Wirth and Mr. Sommerville looked at each other, as if seeking some sort of agreement on buying this explanation.

"What's that?" Mr. Wirth asked, noticing that Adam was about to say something. But Adam had no idea what else to say, even though he sensed that the vagueness of his explanation had not satisfied his interrogators.

Stick to the truth, as much as possible. Don't say too much. It'll only get you into trouble. Adam remembered all of the episodes of *Law & Order* he had watched. *Never give more than they ask for. Tell them your story and stick to it.* Adam could feel sweat collecting under his armpits. A droplet rolled down his shirtsleeve.

"And none of this could wait until office hours, Mr. Proffit?" Mr. Wirth asked authoritatively, as if he did not believe a word of what Adam had said.

"Well, um, to be honest sir, I hadn't planned on going to see Professor Moran at all. I had gotten out of bed 'cause I was tossing and turning. I didn't want to wake Kellum, my roommate, so I just went outside the room to pace the hall."

Adam watched, gauging their reactions. Mr. Wirth leaning in, interestedly, Mr. Sommerville leaning back in his chair as if settling in for the long haul.

"Anyway, I guess I still woke up Kellum. He asked me where I was going, so I just told him the bathroom. I walked around for a while. Then I saw a flashlight, and I knew someone was making rounds."

Mr. Wirth leaned across his desk a little further, as if Adam were about to deliver a punch line.

"I know it was wrong, sir, but I hid behind a door. I was going to go back to my room, but when I saw it was Professor Moran, I went ahead and knocked on his door, since he was awake and all."

"Yes?" Mr. Wirth questioned.

"I know it was poor judgment. I was just so desperate to talk to someone, and this seemed like the right opportunity. I didn't mean to do anything wrong," Adam pleaded.

"I see," Mr. Wirth said, folding his hands in a prayerful position, then resting his chin on his fingers and staring down at his desk. He remained silent.

Adam was certain they could see that he was sweating. He looked at Mr. Wirth as the man contemplated what Adam had said. Adam thought he might explode if no one said anything. He wondered what Mr. Wirth already knew. Maybe Carter had already confessed, spilled out the sordid details of their rendezvous. Adam feared that Mr. Wirth was waiting to trap him in a lie so that there would be a whole different reason to kick him out.

Then he wouldn't have to let anyone know that Melbourne has any gay students, Adam thought suddenly, his heart hammering against his ribs. *Holy shit. He knows. I know he knows. I'm sunk. I'll be lucky to get into a community college. What am I going to tell Dad? Oh God, what am I going to tell Dad?*

"Mr. Proffit," Mr. Wirth began, finally breaking the silence. Adam looked up, his mind reeling. "This is a very sensitive question, and I assume you will use better discretion in answering it than you did late yesterday evening when you visited a faculty member after lights-out. Mr. Proffit, has Professor Moran ever made any advances toward you—and I mean advances of a sexual nature?"

"Uh, no, sir. What would make you ask a question like that?" *Oh God, it's because he knows. It's because he knows.*

"I'll ask the questions here, Mr. Proffit. Has Professor Moran ever done anything, ever said anything to you that might be construed as a sexual overture?"

What did he tell them? Did he blame it on himself? Oh God, this is all my fault. I'm the one who went after him. I'm the one to blame.

"No, sir, never. He's my advisor—and a good one," Adam answered.

"Mr. Proffit," Mr. Wirth began, and then paused, "are you a homosexual?"

What does he think? That I was seduced? That I'm straight and that I was seduced?

"A…what?"

"You heard me, Mr. Proffit. A homosexual, someone who likes boys, men."

"Uh, well, I beg your pardon?" *Where is he going with this? What do I say?*

"Son, don't play games with me. It's a simple question. Are you a homosexual?"

"Well, sir," Adam began, "there are times when I've thought I might be."

"Answer the question, Mr. Proffit."

"I don't know, sir. I have sometimes thought I might be. That's the best I can do." *It was almost true. Kind of true. Were they buying it?* Adam sensed how uncomfortable Mr. Wirth was with the subject matter and hoped that this line of questioning would soon end.

"Have you ever engaged in homosexual acts, Mr. Proffit, with other men?"

"Um, I don't think so, sir."

"Damn it, Mr. Proffit, answer my question!" Mr. Wirth shouted, slamming his fist against his desk, startling Adam so much that he jumped violently in his chair. "Have you ever done it with another man?"

The only thing Adam could think of was President Clinton, how he had managed to skate through scandal after scandal by cleverly playing on words, by evading questions with well-spoken answers, by narrowly defining sex.

"No, sir, I have never done that," Adam answered.

There. I've done it. I've lied. A bold-faced lie. They're going to expel me, tell me to pack my bags today. Oh God, will they be the ones to call Dad, or will I have to? Maybe I can tell Elizabeth. She'll soften the blow. I think she knows or at least suspects.

"Good, because that kind of thing would never be tolerated at Melbourne. Do you understand me?"

"Yessir, yessir, I do."

As nervous as Adam was, a rage began to boil within him from a place he never knew existed. What's so wrong with being gay? Adam suddenly wanted to stand up and scream in Mr. Wirth's face that he sucked cock, that he loved the taste and smell of cum, that although he had never "done it," he could not wait to take it in the ass, do sixty-nine, seventy-one, twenty-two, and just about every other position ever imaginable to explore sexual identity and become fluent in the language of how people love one another. But Adam knew that saying any of this was certain to get him kicked out and get Carter fired.

And it was still possible that they did not know anything. *Keep your cool*, Adam told himself. After all, there were only a few months until graduation, and if he could just get through that time, if he could make it to the end of the semester, everything might fall into place somehow.

"Thank you, Mr. Proffit. That will be all. You can go back to your class until further notice."

With this single sentence, Adam was dismissed and turned to leave the headmaster's office, but not before he overheard Mr. Wirth instructing Mrs. Brockman to "retrieve Mr. Moran."

Retrieve Mr. Moran? I wonder if they even talked to him yet? God, I really fucked this one up, Adam thought, *for me and for Carter.* He thought about finding a corner in which to hide so that he could warn Carter about what he had said and about what he needed to say. But he knew that if he were caught, he would only make things worse.

*   *   *   *

By the time Mason Bird went to collect Carter for the second time, his class had let out, and Carter was looking over papers without much success, too preoccupied with the events of the morning to concentrate on anything but what had happened and the disastrous consequences that would surely follow. These same thoughts kept him occupied all the way back to the headmaster's office, where Mrs. Brockman, again with the same abruptness, instructed him to go in.

"Sit down, Mr. Moran," Mr. Wirth said knowingly. "We've just had a most interesting chat with Mr. Proffit." The headmaster leaned forward behind his desk. "Did you know, Mr. Moran, that Mr. Proffit has wondered whether he might be a homosexual?"

It seemed like such a ridiculous question, Carter thought. For all the pomp and circumstance with which he had been summoned to the headmaster's office, this was not the volatile confrontation he had envisioned, but, to the contrary, it was the question of someone who had no clue about what had happened or even what he was talking about.

"Why, no, sir. Mr. Proffit has never mentioned that to me," Carter replied, trying to remain calm and relaxed.

"Well, he has to me. And let me tell you, Mr. Moran, that allowing such a student into your personal quarters after hours, after lights-out, only creates a liability that the Melbourne School cannot afford to assume."

Carter wanted to smile, to shout, to laugh aloud. *The bastard doesn't know a damn thing! If he did, he wouldn't be talking about Melbourne's liabilities. You stupid, arrogant, fucking bastard!*

"Think, Mr. Moran, how it would look to someone outside this school if even the hint of such a scandal raised its ugly head. Why, our competitor schools would love nothing better than an uproar of this kind, and the tabloids would love it!"

Yeah, I'll bet they would, Carter thought.

"So next time any situation arises, Mr. Moran, that even hints of any kind of impropriety, have the good sense God gave you to get on the telephone and call another faculty member so you can corroborate what happens. I'm going to let you off with a warning, Mr. Moran, and I'm not even going to note this in your file."

What a generous bastard you are.

"We like what we've seen of you. The students like you, and we think you'd make an excellent fit at Melbourne if you decided to return here after you finish Harvard," Mr. Wirth continued. It was the same speech he had given when Carter had arrived, only to a different audience, a different Carter Moran, a less timid and fearful person than he had been upon his arrival at Melbourne.

"I know this hasn't been a pleasant experience, Mr. Moran. But I assure you, every faculty member has made mistakes—not all mistakes of impropriety, but mistakes nonetheless. We take what we do here very seriously, and I hope you'll look at this experience as a positive one."

Yeah, it's been a real thrill, Carter thought with a newfound confidence about who he was.

"It's only because we care so much about our students, our faculty, and this school that we must do everything we can to protect them. I hope you understand, but more important, I hope you can respect that."

You don't deserve my respect, Carter thought savagely. *And the only thing you care about is protecting your image—as if people like me, people like Adam Proffit,*

*would somehow tarnish your image if the truth came out about us. Wouldn't Mel-
bourne be a better place if its students could be themselves instead of molded into what
crusty bastards like you think they should be?*

"Why, yes, certainly," Carter lied.

"That'll be all, then."

"Thank you, sir."

"Oh, but one more thing. I think we should transfer Mr. Proffit to another
faculty advisor. I think he may have some unnatural feelings or ideas about you,
and I'd like to nip them in the bud. I've wondered about that boy before, and
what I learned today more than confirms my suspicions."

"You're not kicking him out, are you?"

"Heavens, no. Do you think I want a damn lawsuit? Not that I wouldn't like
to kick him out—he all but admitted that he was a card-carrying fudge packer.
No place for queers at Melbourne," Mr. Wirth blurted out, losing his customary
decorum.

Carter wanted to lunge across the desk and punch him in the face, knock out
his teeth, turn the hate and force of his words into a parody, remove his fangs so
that the venom of his speech drooled from his gums.

Wirth continued, oblivious to Carter's inner fury and contempt. "But unless I
catch 'em in the act—you know, prove it—there's not a damn thing I can do.
I'm going to keep an eye on Proffit until he graduates. If he so much as looks at
me the wrong way, he'll be packing his bags for home. To think he's such good
friends—roommates, for that matter—with Kellum Thurman, one of our
best-liked students. And I believe you know how good the Thurmans have been
to this school."

*Why wouldn't Adam deserve to be friends with the likes of Kellum Thurman or
any of your other perfect students at this school?* Carter's thoughts pounded through
him, but with great effort, he controlled his body.

"Anyway, it was Kellum who reported him in the first place, so perhaps they're
not such good friends after all. But then, Kellum is a prefect, so friend or no
friend, that was his job."

*Oh my God. Poor Adam. Is this the kind of friendship this school forges, where best
friends stab each other in the back? This place sucks. You don't get it at all, Wirth.
You're not teaching anyone, leading anyone. You're only brainwashing them to be
bigoted old bastards like you.*

Despite the relative poverty in which Carter had grown up, he suddenly felt an
intense sense of well-being, the kind that no amount of money or connections

could buy. He didn't think himself better for it, just grateful, liberated from the superficial strictures of people like Wirth.

Carter's anger toward Wirth suddenly evolved into a benign sympathy for people like him who were so caught up in pride and material thoughts that they could never experience or understand the exquisite elation of holding their minds open to the world of ideas and possibilities.

"Yes, sir. Anything else?"

"Nope, that's it. I'm glad we could clear up this little matter."

"Thank you, sir," Carter said, then shook hands again with Mr. Wirth and Mr. Sommerville.

As he walked back to his apartment, Carter felt nauseated and, yes, still angry. All the things Mr. Wirth had said about Adam made him want to light a match to the Monroe Building and everything it stood for. *And poor Adam*, Carter thought, *turned in by his own roommate. What kind of place is this school?* But at least the confrontations had not turned out as badly as they could have. He and Adam could bide their time until graduation and then never set foot on Melbourne's campus again.

CHAPTER 23

▼

LONG DISTANCE

The next several weeks seemed to pass without incident. By Mr. Wirth's immediate order, Adam was transferred to another faculty advisor, and Carter saw him only in class, where they barely spoke to each other. But not a class went by during which Adam did not look at Carter longingly, though his yearning had more to do with losing the intimacy of their friendship than with the one night of passion, when they both had lost themselves in the moment.

Carter heard through the grapevine that Adam would likely be accepted at several top colleges, including Princeton, Yale, and Duke. He wanted to take Adam aside and congratulate him, to ask about his plans but also, more importantly, about how he was doing.

Then there was the lingering issue of knowing that Kellum Thurman, Adam's roommate, had started the whole mess in the first place. Carter wondered what could have motivated Kellum to do such a thing. Of course, there was the Honor Code, but Carter found it hard to believe that the Code alone had been Kellum's sole motivation to betray the trust of a close friend. Carter knew that what had happened between Adam and him was wrong, but he had accepted the fact that their passion had been a mistake of happenstance and weakness, instead of the result of lurid or seedy intentions.

Carter must have read through Adam's term paper ten times, admiring his prose, his clever use of organization, and his inventive use of syntax as he bent the rules of Strunk and White in ways they were meant to be broken. The attraction

Carter had felt for Adam had turned into pure fondness and admiration of a beautiful young man with a strong mind and a lively spirit. Adam was, after all, much like the fabled pelican in his mother's stories. His strength and character would take him through Melbourne and on to many new adventures, which Carter hoped would be rewarding.

Carter also hoped that one day, when Adam looked back on it all, he would not resent Carter and would remember him for being a vulnerable person as much in need of love and friendship as was Adam himself. Carter hated the thought of ending such a glorious friendship simply because Mr. Wirth and the rest of the administration were too small-minded to allow contact between them. *If they only knew what really happened,* Carter thought, *it would blow their fucking minds.* But theirs was not a story he would ever repeat.

He looked at the stack of term papers he had finished grading, his handwriting scribbled across the pages, his comments ranging from high praise to constructive criticism. All the papers had been impressive. And it occurred to him that Melbourne was doing at least some things right.

CHAPTER 24

▼

AN ALLY

The spring morning was beautiful, crisp, and clear. Carter had climbed onto the roof of the Monroe Building to watch the sun rise above the Blue Ridge Mountains. When he had first discovered the roof location, he could not help but smile at all the discarded cigarette butts that had collected at the intersection of the rooflines between the main building and its west wing. He wondered how many generations of Melbourne students had crawled out onto the ancient slate roof of the building and up to the highest point to smoke a cigarette or to catch the sun rising or setting—truly the most beautiful Carter had ever seen. He looked down at his watch. It was six thirty. He still had plenty of time to get ready for the brunch reception being held for the Melbourne trustees later in the morning.

Carter wondered whether the Fitz-Warings would be there, pulling themselves away from whatever else people with their resources did to attend a brunch reception at the small country school to which they had contributed liberally. Carter hoped they would attend. Even if he did not have the courage to talk to them, he was curious to see what they looked like. After reading *The Ties That Bind*, Carter felt that he had seen into Mrs. Fitz-Waring's soul, and he was eager to see for himself what she looked like and how her social persona might differ from or conform to the self-portrait she had painted in her autobiographical account of the time when her son had first told her he was gay.

*   *   *   *

Carter had just showered and now pulled from the closet the Haspel tan pop-lin suit he had purchased from Perlis in New Orleans before making the drive to Melbourne. He put on the freshly ironed white shirt, purchased during the same trip, and the Melbourne rep tie from the student commissary. Glancing in the mirror, he was surprised by how handsome he looked. He thought about how proud his mother would be to see him dressed in a suit, like a real professional.

He and his mother had not spoken in several weeks. Carter had avoided her calls and had not bothered to call her back. He was too afraid that when she asked how he was doing, he might break down and tell her what had happened with Adam and with the school administration. Not ever having confided his sex-uality to her, he knew that information would be too much for her to take in over the phone, certainly more than he thought she could even begin to understand.

Carter stepped out of his apartment and locked the door.

"Hey, lookin' pretty dapper there, Professor. Got a date?" one of the students asked, then laughed as he turned to whisper into another student's ear.

"No, just a reception. And, by the way, whispering is impolite," Carter reproached him.

"Sorry, Professor, didn't mean to be rude."

"Not to worry," Carter replied. "Just try to remember next time that whisper-ing in the company of others only raises the presumption that you're saying unkind things about them. While possibly tolerated among eight-year-old girls, it's not the kind of behavior you should continue at Melbourne."

"Yessir," the student replied, with his head slightly down.

When Carter stepped into Lampton Hall, where the brunch was to take place, most of the other faculty had already arrived. One of the most elegant buildings on the Melbourne campus, Lampton Hall had been built as a library in the 1890s by the grandson of the Earl of Durham, a branch of the family that had settled in the United States after the earl's son married the heiress to a mercantile fortune. When the school eventually needed a larger library, Lampton Hall was chosen to house the school's burgeoning collection of historical documents, along with fine furniture and other such donations that Melbourne had accumulated over the years. The grand, formal rooms of the building were the most ornate interiors at the school and stood in stark contrast to the clean-lined, classically restrained Vir-ginia architecture that predominated the campus.

Carter stepped from the hallway into the vaulted reception room, with its stone walls and gothic arched windows. A pair of massive iron chandeliers softly lit the interior. Waiters were busily checking the enormous chafing dishes lined up on long tables at either side of the huge receiving room. Other waiters were carrying trays of Bloody Marys and mimosas.

"Well, there you are, Mr. Moran," Shasta Brockman said in the same friendly tone she had always used, except for the time when Carter was being interrogated by Mr. Wirth. She took a large sip from her Bloody Mary and continued, "I was worried you might not be coming."

"I would not have missed it for the world. The food at these things is so much better than what we're used to in the cafeteria."

"Isn't that the truth? And the drinks are pretty good too."

"Yup," Carter agreed. "Hey, Mrs. Brockman, do you know if the Fitz-Warings are here?"

"Now, you know better than to call me Mrs. Brockman. I've told you, call me Shasta. It makes me feel so old when even the faculty members call me Mrs. Brockman, especially when the faculty are as young and handsome as you. Why, if I were younger, I don't think I'd let you out of my sight."

Carter could tell that Shasta Brockman had probably already met her quota of Bloody Marys, but then, who was he to raise eyebrows at anyone's behavior? He wondered what the old gal was like when she really got to drinking, and he made a personal bet that she might exceed that quota today given the start she'd apparently had.

"You flatter me, Shasta," Carter said.

"Now, that's better, and, by the way, my offer still stands to introduce you to some of our loverly Fauquier County girls." She took another drink of her Bloody Mary and said, "What were you asking me about?"

"The Fitz-Warings. Do you know if they're here?"

"They are. Why do you ask?"

"Well, uh…" Carter began.

"I know. You are gonna try your hand at networking. Good show." Shasta Brockman finished off the remains of her Bloody Mary through the tiny cocktail straw, causing a high-pitched suction sound. "Oops," she giggled and clumsily discarded the glass on the tray of a passing waiter before quickly grabbing, and almost dropping, a fresh drink from the same waiter's tray.

"Oh, that will make Mr. Wirth so happy to know that you're taking an interest in school development. So many of the faculty have no interest in it at all or aren't any good at it," Shasta continued with a slight slur. "But with your good looks, I'll bet you could charm any of our trustees into doubling the size of the Monroe Building."

"Well, I want to do my part," Carter replied.

"Let me see," Shasta Brockman said as she looked around the room. "There they are, talking to Professor Caruthers. He'll bore them to death. Why, five minutes with him and you'd want to jump off the Rappahannock Bridge! Come on, Carter. I'll introduce you."

With this, Shasta Brockman scurried across the room, clutching the sleeve of Carter's jacket like a wild eagle carrying its kill to the nest.

"Oh, Mr. and Mrs. Fitz-Waring," Shasta Brockman interrupted with a long slur. "I have someone I am dying for you to meet. This is our newest and youngest faculty member, Carter Moran. We have him for only a year, and then," Shasta whispered, "he's off to Harvard. But we're going to try and get him back when he finishes. Melbourne could use some new blood, don't you think, Mr. Caruthers?" Shasta Brockman dropped Carter's sleeve to clutch Mr. Caruthers by the arm. She led him away, brushing some of the dandruff from the back of his jacket.

"Well, it's a pleasure to meet you Mr. Moran," Mrs. Fitz-Waring said, extending her hand to Carter. "I'm Elaine, and this is my husband, Jack."

"It's a pleasure to meet you both," Carter began. "I can't tell you how much your support has meant to the school." Carter realized that this was probably the same drivel the Fitz-Warings had heard hundreds of times from Melbourne's administrators and faculty.

"Oh, look," Jack Fitz-Waring said, "there's Ben Moore. Will you excuse me, Mr. Moran? I need to go say hello. It was a pleasure meeting you. Elaine, do you mind?"

"Not at all," Elaine Fitz-Waring replied. "Go right on ahead."

Elaine Fitz-Waring placed her hand gently on Carter's shoulder. "How are you liking Melbourne?" she asked.

"I do like it, very much," said Carter. He looked closely at Mrs. Fitz-Waring as he spoke, noticing that she looked younger than he had imagined, her eyes almost unlined and very gentle. She had straight brown hair curled under and pulled behind her ears. She was elegantly dressed in a key-lime knit suit with low-heeled shoes and a small Chanel handbag.

Carter added, "What this school does for the boys is nothing short of wonderful. I grew up a poor kid from Mississippi, so I am still amazed by all the opportunities the students have here. Still, there are some students I worry about."

"And which students are those?" Elaine Fitz-Waring asked with a concerned look suggesting that, unlike many of the polite conversations that accompanied functions involving the trustees, this conversation might genuinely interest her.

Recalling her book, Carter remembered her eloquence in describing the emotions that had poured through her when her son first told her he was gay—first resentment, then hostility and self-reproach, and, finally, understanding and acceptance.

"Well, Mrs. Fitz-Waring, may I speak candidly with you?"

"Yes, of course, and please call me Elaine," she said, gently squeezing the bend of Carter's arm, which she had not yet released.

"Thank you, Elaine. I wanted to tell you how deeply I was moved by your book, *The Ties That Bind*," Carter began.

This comment prompted Elaine Fitz-Waring to look around the room and then step a little closer to Carter.

"I take it no one at Melbourne has ever mentioned your book to you before?" Carter asked.

"No, and not that I'm ashamed of what I wrote, but as much as we love the school, it's still a bit closed-minded for my taste. How, may I ask, did you come to read my book, Carter?"

It was a loaded question. But she was such a graceful woman, and her eyes seemed so kind, that Carter dared to continue. He hoped that he might be providing her with an opportunity that she had perhaps been hoping for—to help make Melbourne a less conservative place.

"Well, let's just say, I have something in common with one of your sons," Carter replied.

Elaine smiled and nodded. "Oh, you are very clever, Carter. I certainly like that." She looked briefly around the room again. "Well, let me ask you this," she said. "The students that you're concerned about—do they also have something in common with you and my son?"

"Very perceptive, Elaine. I knew I liked you."

"Likewise, Carter. So what are you proposing?"

"At this point, I'm not in a position to propose anything. Much of this world at Melbourne is very new to me. I'm not sure what would need to be done—or could be done—to help make Melbourne a better place for people like me, but more importantly, like your son."

"And you worry about the other students."

"That's correct."

"Well. It's something that I have thought about many times, Carter, many times. It's a big problem to tackle. On the one hand, a place like Melbourne has wonderful traditions and values that should be cherished and preserved. But all that history is accompanied by the dead weight of some very outdated and old-fashioned ideals that tend to stifle open-minded thought and self-expression. It's hard to know how not to throw the baby out with the bathwater, so to speak."

"Exactly," Carter agreed.

"I take it I'm pretty safe in assuming that no one here knows that you are…like one of my sons," Elaine asked.

"Very safe," Carter replied.

"Well, unfortunately, it's probably best to keep it that way, at least for the time being. But I would be very interested in talking to you about this further. My husband and I are both very active in PFLAG. You're familiar with the organization?"

"Yes."

Elaine leaned a bit closer to Carter. "You and I are coming from a different place than some of the other people involved. Some parents and administrators are very, very conservative. Others are more moderate. And then there are parents more like my husband and me. Sometimes I feel that we're caught between our time-honored traditions, which make us who we are, and our ideals and convictions about loving our children and improving the world for them. While Melbourne is a wonderful school for some boys, I think it could be very difficult for others. It's hard to know how to fix it without changing it—possibly for the better but possibly for the worse."

"I know exactly what you mean," said Carter, understanding the difficulty immediately.

"Well, listen, here is my card," Elaine Fitz-Waring said, handing him a calling card from her handbag. "You call me any time. And I'll do the same. I'd better go catch up with Jack. It looks like Old Caruthers has glommed onto him again. I'm so glad that Shasta introduced us!" Elaine Fitz-Waring stood on her tiptoes and kissed Carter on the cheek.

"Me too," Carter replied, and then he watched her admiringly as she walked gracefully across the room to reclaim her husband.

*   *   *   *

Adam took deliberately slow steps from the soccer field, watching Kellum make his way up the hill and talk jovially to some of the other players. It felt alienating not to be at his side. Other students had to notice. For so long, Adam and Kellum had been inseparable. But now Kellum did everything he could to avoid being around Adam.

What could he be thinking? Adam wondered. *How many of the details of the incident with Professor Moran does he know, if anything?* Facts about investigations into student conduct were not usually disclosed to the prefects unless the Prefect Board was called into session, and the board had not been convened following Adam's interrogation by Mr. Wirth. There had been no trial, no indictment. Mr. Wirth had used his prosecutorial discretion and not pressed charges against Adam, for lack of evidence—or no evidence at all, as far as Adam knew.

Adam wondered how the whole interrogation had begun in the first place. As best as he could remember, no one had seen him leaving his room that night. No one had seen him enter or leave Carter's apartment. Kellum was the only person who knew he had left their dorm room, but Adam was certain that he would not have said anything.

Adam looked back up the hill at the closest friend he had ever had, one who no longer wanted anything to do with him, and wondered for the first time whether Kellum had been involved in turning him in.

Nah, Adam thought. *He's probably just heard the rumors. Probably freaked out about it. Nobody wants anything to do with a faggot like me.*

CHAPTER 25

▼

A DIFFERENT PLACE

"Hey," Adam asked. "Want to go to the Rapp?"

"Nah. Thanks, though," Kellum replied, returning his attention to the book he was reading.

"All right, then," Adam said despondently. "See ya later."

"Yeah, later."

During the weeks following his interrogation by Mr. Wirth, it seemed that it wasn't just Kellum avoiding him but also a number of other students. Adam had noticed this change first among the Sixth Formers, then the Fifth, the Fourth, and finally the Third Formers. The cause was not difficult to figure out. Melbourne was small, and after word of what had happened—or what had been suggested as having happened—began to spread through the various cliques of the school, Adam soon began feeling like an untouchable.

It was as if he had been transported back to camp, when he was a boy and had been made an outcast by a one-time incident with another camper, an incident that Adam had not instigated and about which he had told no one. That incident had been turned against him by the very same camper who had solicited Adam in the first place. The only difference was that Adam knew Carter had not told anyone, that Carter had not betrayed him like the camper whose lies had tainted Adam's existence throughout his secondary education until he'd arrived at Melbourne.

But Adam's alienation from Kellum gouged deeply into his long-dormant wounds, causing pangs of sadness, loneliness, and horrific regret to cut through him like the dull, rusty blade of a past he had long since tried to forget.

Serves me right, Adam thought, remembering what he had done in their New York hotel room. *I am a pervert. I deserve to be persecuted. I deserve to die.*

If only Kellum were sticking by him, everything would be different. By this time, Adam no longer cared what anyone else at Melbourne thought of him, including Mr. Wirth, Mr. Sommerville, the prefects, and the rest of the student body. Carter and Kellum were the only people he cared about. But he was all but forbidden to see Carter, and there seemed little chance of resurrecting his friendship with Kellum.

$$* \qquad * \qquad * \qquad *$$

Adam sat alone in the booth at the Rapp where he and Kellum usually sat, looking down at the onion rings and Coke he had ordered but for which he had no appetite. *This is the worst place I could have come*, he thought, although there seemed nowhere else to go. He certainly could not go to his dorm room, even though Kellum probably was not there anyway. Kellum avoided being anywhere close to Adam until lights-out, when he would arrive and go directly to sleep after an obligatory "Good night," which Kellum was too well mannered not to say.

Adam got up from the booth and tossed the uneaten onion rings and full cup of Coke into the trash can.

"Everything OK, baby?" Big Aggie inquired. "Looks like you didn't eat a bite."

"Oh, fine, Big Aggie. My eyes were just bigger than my stomach."

"Oh, Lord, wish I had that problem, but then I guess I'd be Skinny Aggie instead of ole Big Aggie."

"You're perfect just the way you are, Aggie, just the way you are."

"Now that's my baby. I'm going to miss you when you graduate. Some come and others go, but I'm gonna miss you."

"I'll miss you too, Big Aggie. I'll miss you a lot."

Adam smiled at her, trying not to burst into a million pieces, then rounded the corner of the Rapp, where he looked around to see if anyone was in sight. He leaned against the wall, bent down, and began inhaling and exhaling deeply, the way he did before a track meet. After several deep breaths, when he felt that he had regained his composure, he walked down the long, narrow corridor at the bottom of the Monroe Building to the other side, where the student mailboxes were housed, across from the commissary. As he passed, Adam could see a parcel shading the small window of his mailbox. *Probably another postcard from Dad and Elizabeth*, he thought as he unlocked the mailbox and pulled out a large envelope with the Princeton insignia on the return address.

Adam's heart raced as he looked at the thick parcel. He locked his mailbox and darted out the west doors of the building, which led directly to Agony Hill, the three-mile incline up to the side entrance of the building. Agony Hill had earned its name because it usually made up the last three miles of the long-distance training runs for members of the track and cross-country teams like Adam. After five-and six-mile runs, the last three miles up to the school followed the long, slow incline of Agony Hill.

Adam took off, running down Agony Hill like a zephyr, faster and faster, pushing harder and harder, as if he could somehow outrun everything he was feeling, everything that was making him lonely and miserable. When he reached the bottom of Agony Hill, he darted toward the Melbourne countryside, which he knew so well from all his years of training. He sped through the fields, then the woods, deeper and deeper, until he reached a plateau overlooking the Rappahannock River that he had never discovered before.

There was no telling how many miles he had run, the envelope in his hand now wrinkled and damp from sweat. He knelt down and breathed in and out deeply, as he had done in the Monroe Building not long before. Then he sat on the plateau overlooking the river and listened to the sound of water gushing along below him. He looked across the river into the dense thicket of vegetation that seemed to have no end.

As he sat there, alone in the wilderness, he felt for the first time in weeks that everything was going to be all right. No matter what happened, he would be all right too. He had been through the same kind of trouble before, and he would get through it again. And whether he held an acceptance or a rejection did not seem to matter. He would survive, regardless of where he went from the place he had found within himself. "Well, Princeton," Adam said softly, "if you don't want me, I can always go to LSU."

Adam began to peel open the soggy envelope, which was already half-unsealed from the perspiration that had soaked into the paper. He pulled out the now damp contents, his hands shaking, and unfolded them, looked up into the sky, and finally looked down at the sparsely written lines that specified at least one part of his future:

Dear Mr. Proffit:

We are pleased to offer you admission to Princeton University. Additional information will follow, including further orientation, housing, and detailed course material. You will be assigned a faculty advisor upon your arrival at the campus.

Please review the enclosed materials, noting that you will need to return your acceptance within the specified deadline. You will also find enclosed some of the details of the full Wilton P. Laird Scholarship that you have been awarded.

Please do not hesitate to contact the undersigned if you have any questions regarding your admission.

We look forward to hearing from you and to having you here with us at Princeton. Congratulations!

Sincerely,

Jane Weir, Admissions

"Yahooo!" Adam screamed as loudly as he could into the woods, jumping up and down, still clutching the soggy materials from Princeton. When he had finally calmed down, he stopped, looked up into the sky, and said softly, "Thank you, God! I won't disappoint you!"

CHAPTER 26

▼

BREAKING THE ICE

After returning from the far corners of Melbourne's campus, Adam felt completely uplifted and changed. Any awkward stares or innuendo would no longer bother him, would not rip into the old wounds of his past, and would not stop him from being the person he was. He would be the same likable Adam that he had been before anything had started, only more confident, less reticent, and more comfortable with himself, because he just did not give a damn. He was leaving Melbourne and going to Princeton, and whether he went with or without the support of his friends no longer mattered.

Adam left the cafeteria line carrying his lunch tray and walked over toward the prefects' table, where Kellum and six of the other prefects, including Birdy, were huddled to one side of the table. Adam had not sat with them in weeks, eating most of his meals at the Rapp. He sensed an awkward silence as he approached the table, set down his tray, and pulled out a chair.

"What, did somebody die or something?" Adam asked.

"Hey, who invited you here, Proffit?" Birdy asked.

"I didn't think I needed to be invited, Birdy. I've been sitting with you guys all year. If I'm unwelcome, I'd sure like to know it. Well, Birdy? Am I unwelcome?"

"Nah, 'course not, Proffit. But it wouldn't seem right if I didn't give you any shit."

"Back at ya, Birdy. Back at ya," Adam replied.

"So, Willoughby, was that your sister I saw you with last weekend?" one of the other prefects, Charles Drummond, asked another boy.

"Nah, that's his new girlfriend from Sarah Walker," another chimed in.

"So, like I said, was that your sister, Willoughby?" Drummond retorted, prompting laughter from the rest of the table.

"No, I'm not from West Virginia like you, Drummond, so we don't do that kind of thing," Esmond Willoughby replied.

"You sure about that? 'Cause your mom's eyes are kind of close together. Got a real *Deliverance* look about her."

More laughter from around the table.

"So, Willoughby, Sarah Walker? Sure she's not a carpet muncher? I hear all those girls are lesbians," Drummond continued.

"And you have a problem with that?"

"No. Actually I think it's hot. But you're such a fag, Willoughby. You wouldn't know what to do with a lesbian if she landed on your face. Oops, no offense, Proffit," Drummond said sarcastically.

"None taken. I've had many lesbians land on my face. Nothing to it," Adam replied, prompting more laughter from the table.

It was the first semi-normal interaction that Adam had had with any of the prefects since the incident with Professor Moran had caused almost everything to change. Much to Adam's surprise, the group seemed almost relieved to end the awkward and uncomfortable silence between them and to return things to more or less normal—despite the suggestion in Drummond's comment that Adam was a fag, which Adam decided to take as a signal that they knew what was being said about him, but that it was OK. While Drummond may have expected Adam to address the remark with a pithy retort about his sexuality, Adam was not yet ready to go that far with it and had not thought of anything else to say.

$$\ast \qquad \ast \qquad \ast \qquad \ast$$

"You were kind of on a roll today at lunch," Kellum said to Adam just after lights-out, making one of the first attempts at any form of conversation in several weeks.

"Not really," Adam replied.

"Well, it was good to have you back, buddy."

"Thanks, good to be back."

"Good night."

"Night."

Although the exchange was brief, Adam began to realize that perhaps much of the isolation he had been feeling was, at least to some extent, self-imposed. While he was certain that people had been acting differently toward him, he realized that he had probably been avoiding people as much as they had been avoiding him.

CHAPTER 27

▼

RECKONING

It was the Saturday before graduation, just after lights-out, when Adam broached a subject that he and Kellum had never discussed.

"Kellum, you awake?"

"Yeah, what is it?"

"How come you never told me?"

"Never told you what?"

"That you were the one, the one who turned me in."

Adam had not expected such complete silence. It was a rhetorical question, after all, but he had expected Kellum to say something—although his silence spoke volumes. After reconstructing the events of the past several months over and over again, Adam clearly realized that Kellum was the only person who could have turned him in. No one else had seen him leave the room. No one else had seen him that night at all. Kellum was the only person who knew when he had left their room and how long he was gone.

After the school had finally settled down, after the rumors had subsided, after the other students and the faculty had stopped making awkward glances, and after Adam had re-injected himself into his old life at Melbourne, Kellum had never again mentioned anything about going to the same college or rooming together—or anything that would remotely suggest that their friendship would continue after graduation. Lately, Kellum had been pleasant enough, trying not to show that anything had changed, wearing the same mask that stoically concealed the person beneath. Adam wondered whether he had ever really known Kellum at all, whether the golden boy whom he had loved and admired was nothing more than an illusion that Kellum so artfully projected into the world, wondered whether even Kellum knew what was real about himself and what was not.

Now the silence in their room was broken by the unmistakable sound of Kellum trying to conceal his sobs. Adam remembered the night he had been with Carter, then remembered how much resentment he had felt toward Kellum, who, after four years of being friends, had chosen that particular occasion to open up to him about whatever it was he needed to say. Apparently this was how things would always be between Adam and Kellum—too little too late.

"Adam," Kellum finally said, in the broken, dispirited voice of someone other than Kellum Thurman, the golden-boy prefect. "I'm sorry. I'm very, very sorry."

Adam felt more irritated than angry. While he had raised the issue, his question had been only a way of apprising Kellum of the fact that Adam knew what he had done. Why Kellum had done it was irrelevant, as far as Adam was concerned. "Yeah," Adam replied, "well, sorry doesn't cut it, couldn't even begin to cut it." He turned on his side, facing the wall, as if to go to sleep.

"Adam?"

"What? What the fuck is it?"

"Can you ever forgive me?"

Adam could feel his blood pressure igniting, flaring through his temples, as if he might explode.

"Why the fuck would I want to do that? Give me one good reason, just one."

There was a long silence before Adam could hear Kellum break into tears, louder and less controlled. "Because you're my best friend, and I love you."

Adam was steaming. He sat up in his bed. "What does turning me in have to do with friendship? And what the hell could you possibly know about love? Do you even know that I fucking loved you, ached over you for three goddamn years? Do you know that as crazy as your jokes and teasing made me, I put up with it all because I couldn't stand the thought of not being around you?"

At this point, Adam had no reason to hold back. He had been accepted to Princeton, he had lost his friendship with Kellum, and nothing would prevent him from finally telling the truth. It was like releasing a cancer that had been eating away his insides for as long as he could remember.

Adam continued, "I would have taken a bullet for you, would have gotten myself kicked out before I ever did anything to hurt you. That's what love is, you motherfucker, that's what love is."

This monologue was followed by a loud pounding on the wall, followed by a muffled "Keep it down, ladies."

For the first time in weeks, Adam began to laugh, and he laughed uncontrollably. No doubt everyone on both sides of the room had heard every word he had said in the same loud, muffled voice as the "Keep it down, ladies" that had just echoed through the wall. But Adam did not care what anyone at Melbourne thought, including Kellum. For the first time since he had been with Carter, he felt completely free. The whole world could know, and he just did not give a damn.

"What's so goddamn funny, Proffit?" Kellum asked, his voice drenched in mucus.

"The whole goddamn fucking thing is funny, that's what."

"You just told me you loved me," Kellum continued. He got up from his bed and blew his nose. Then he knelt down at the side of the lower bunk, where Adam's back was facing him.

"Adam, this scares the crap out of me. I've been so damn confused. When I said I love you, I *do* love you. But I'm just not sure I love you in that way. Maybe I do. Living in this damn fishbowl has me so damn confused, I can hardly think straight."

"That's a good one," Adam chuckled, still feeling unconnected to Kellum and whatever point he was trying to make.

"Listen, if you know who you are, that's fantastic, but give the slow students at the back of the class a little credit," Kellum said. "I don't give a damn what anyone is saying about you, saying about *me* for that matter. I love you, Adam Proffit, and that scares the absolute ever-living crap out of me, because I don't know what the hell I'm supposed to do about it. If you want me to scream it out loud for everyone to hear, I will. *I love you, Adam Proffit!*" Kellum screamed into the room.

More pounding came from both sides of the walls, this time followed by a muffled "Keep it to yourselves. The straight students are trying to sleep."

This prompted more waves of laughter from Adam.

Kellum grabbed Adam's shoulder. "Look at me," he whispered. "Please, just look at me."

Adam turned around and saw a Kellum he had never seen before, brimming with fear, passionate but confused, his teary eyes a well of emotion.

"I goddamn love you. And yes, I turned you in, but I was so damn confused, so damn jealous, I mean—"

"You were jealous?" Adam asked, smiling at Kellum for the first time.

"Yeah, you motherfucker, jealous. OK?"

Adam sat up in bed next to his roommate and placed his hand on Kellum's neck. It was not a playful gesture or even the innuendo-riddled posturing that had for so long been a mark of their friendship. It was a genuine sign of affection.

"Hold me, please," Kellum asked quietly.

Adam took Kellum into his arms and held him tightly. At first Kellum seemed reticent to reciprocate fully, but the tighter Adam held him, the more Adam could feel all of his own anger and resentment melt from within. All Adam felt for Kellum was love, the love he had always had for him, buried deeply within him and finally emerging from the farthest reaches of his being like a phoenix rising from the ashes.

Kellum embraced him more tightly, holding him as closely as possible, as if letting go would cause him to fall into a black hole. Then Kellum pulled away slightly and looked into Adam's eyes, which he studied intently. "I'm not sure what it means," Kellum pleaded gently, "to love another man."

Adam's hands glided up Kellum's spine to the back of his neck, and he pulled Kellum toward him until their lips met and pressed together firmly. Their mouths opened, and their tongues found each other. Kellum gasped slightly, still afraid of what was happening. He could feel himself becoming aroused, terrified of what it meant.

"It's OK," Adam whispered to him gently, kissing the lobe of his ear, then making his way around Kellum's face and back to his mouth, where Kellum's lips embraced his eagerly. They peeled off their shirts, and Kellum found himself lying on top of Adam, looking into his eyes, pressing himself firmly against him. Adam's hands ran down Kellum's back to just under the waistband of his boxer shorts.

"I love you, Adam Proffit. I've always loved you. I just never knew how to say it or what to do about it," Kellum whispered.

"Just kiss me," Adam responded.

Kellum leaned into Adam and kissed him as their hands journeyed across each other's bodies, passionately, gently, vigorously, shedding the remaining layers of clothing so that they were naked, unshielded, lying totally with each other, bursting with emotion. And within the darkness of their dorm room, Adam leaned back and pulled Kellum toward him. Their tongues met, and their bodies moved in rhythmic union, reciting years of unspoken verse about everything they felt for each other.

Kellum looked into Adam's eyes again and whispered, "I love you, Adam Proffit. I love you."

CHAPTER 28

▼

GRADUATING

It was a clear, beautiful day for graduation. All the students were dressed in tropical-weight, grey flannel pants, white oxford shirts, blue and green Melbourne rep ties, and navy jackets with the school insignia.

"And this is my father and stepmother, Walt and Elizabeth Proffit," Adam began the introductions.

Adam was amused by the contrast between his parents and the Thurmans. Elizabeth Proffit had undoubtedly chosen the expensive designer suit that Walt Proffit was sporting, as well as his shirt, tie, socks, and shoes. Elizabeth herself was decked out in an elegant knit suit with several strands of pearls and a wide-brimmed hat, as if she were going to the Kentucky Derby. In contrast, the Thurmans looked more like they had just come from a casual lunch at their club in Palm Beach or some other fashionable location.

But regardless of his clothing, Adam's father had made the trip up to Virginia, and he seemed proud that his son was graduating from such a fine school as Melbourne. "Pleasure to meet you," he said, extending his hand to Mrs. Thurman and shaking it vigorously. This also amused Adam because Kellum had long ago explained that it was improper for a man to extend his hand to a lady unless and until she offered hers first. But in the customary Thurman way, Mrs. Thurman handled the gaffe as if this were the way it was always done.

"Oh, how wonderful it is to meet you both," Upshire Thurman began in her languorous drawl. "I can't tell you how much we cherish your son. He's an absolute delight. And I'm so proud of both of the boys for getting into Princeton. It's going to be wonderful for them. And Adam as valedictorian—you've got to be so proud of your son."

There had been more than one argument between Adam and his father about his decision not to go to Duke, but in the end Adam had won, if only by demonstrating his resolve to stick by his decision. But then, this was the kind of resolve that Walt Proffit had always wanted his son to have, the kind of resolve that had made Walt Proffit—who had never gone to college—successful in business and able to afford the high tuition at Melbourne.

After the Proffits and the Thurmans had made polite conversation, Adam spotted Carter through the corner of his eye. "Can you excuse us for just a second? There's someone I need Dad and Elizabeth to meet."

Adam escorted his father and stepmother to the spot where Carter had just finished greeting another student's parents.

"Um, Professor Moran, this is my father, Walt, and stepmother, Elizabeth— the Proffits."

The conversation lasted only a minute or two, long enough for Carter to congratulate the Proffits on Adam's successes at Melbourne and on his acceptance to Princeton. The exchange caught the attention of a few nearby faculty members, but neither Carter nor Adam cared. But before they walked away, Carter shook Adam's hand and smiled.

"I'm very proud of you, Adam. I'm looking forward to seeing you do great things, great things."

"Thanks, Professor," Adam replied. "Thanks for everything."

The exchange was brief but enough to normalize things after so many awkward months of not being able to speak to each other.

"Take care of yourself."

"You too," Adam replied, then walked away with his parents to where Kellum and the rest of the Thurmans were standing.

"Should I be jealous?" Kellum whispered into Adam's ear.

"Not a bit," Adam whispered back. "Not a bit."

CHAPTER 29

▼

THE BEST AND BRIGHTEST

The faculty were seated to the side of the stage in white wooden chairs, and Jake Sommerville stood behind the podium, officiating over the ceremony. Parents were seated in long rows facing the stage. Crowds of other proud parents and guests stood on either side of them.

"And now, ladies and gentlemen, I'd like to introduce the valedictorian for this year's graduating class, Adam Proffit, who has a few words for you. Adam graduates this year with a four-point average and will be attending Princeton this fall, where he plans to major in English literature. Without further ado, I give you Adam Proffit."

Adam had been dreading this moment. After all that had happened during the last several months, after all the rumors and innuendo, he wondered whether he would be booed off the stage. But much to his surprise, when Mr. Sommerville finished his introduction, waves of applause, wild catcalls, and joyful howls exploded from the student section of the audience. Adam fought back the urge to cry. He suddenly felt cleansed, absolved, and accepted. As he walked across the stage and up to the podium, the noise only became louder. Tears came to his eyes.

"Wow," he said, after reaching the podium. "I think I just realized how much I'm going to miss you guys, no matter how loud and obnoxious you are."

The audience laughed politely, followed by a few more catcalls and cheers from the student section. Then Adam began his speech:

I'm overwhelmed. I've been here four years with most of you. Others, three. But as I stand here, I realize how much I've learned from you while I've been here. Those of you who know me well probably know that I'll be the first person in my family to go to college. It was pretty daunting for me when I first got here, a kid from the wrong side of the tracks down in Louisiana, whose father has worked very hard and has done very well for himself, well enough to send me up here with you.

Anyway, as much as I hope to learn after I leave here, I think the lessons of the past four years have been, and will continue to be, the greatest ones of my life. These are the lessons that have made me the person I will become when I leave here. And I want to thank every person in the student body and in the faculty for making these lessons real and meaningful and purposeful. I stand here eager to begin the future that you have afforded me, but sad at the same time to be leaving you. I know I will see you again, and until then, congratulations to you all. I'll miss you.

Adam waved to his classmates as he walked off the stage, and he was once again astounded as the students rose from their chairs in a standing ovation led by Kellum, who had been sitting in the back with other seniors whose last names began with T. The students continued to applaud and howl as Adam returned to his seat. Someone reached over and messed his hair as he walked by. Another student said, "Way to go, Proffit, great speech!" Adam blushed with pride, overwhelmed and elated.

*   *   *   *

After all the awards had been given and the diplomas passed out, the students left their seats and regrouped with their parents. Adam had just found his father and stepmother when he felt a tap on the shoulder. He turned around to see Mr. Wirth standing there, smiling.

"Mr. Proffit. Wonderful speech. Aren't you going to introduce me to your proud parents?" Mr. Wirth said.

"Oh, yes. Thank you, Mr. Wirth. This is my father, Walt, and stepmother, Elizabeth Proffit."

"Congratulations, Mr. and Mrs. Proffit. We are very proud of Adam, very proud. And I just wanted to come over and congratulate you in person. Wonderful day."

"Thank you," Adam's father said, shaking the headmaster's hand. "Yes, we're very proud of Adam too."

"And you have every reason to be. Anyway, I won't take more of your time. Again, a pleasure to meet you. Congratulations."

Mr. Wirth had just spotted another set of parents whom he hoped to solicit for the endowment when Carter tapped the headmaster on the shoulder.

"Oh, yes, Mr. Moran, what can I do for you?" Mr. Wirth asked.

"That was a nice thing you just said to the Proffits."

"And?" Mr. Wirth asked.

"Did you mean a word of it?"

"What do you mean? Of course I did. What is this about? I don't have time for this." Mr. Wirth looked into the distant crowd of guests to suggest that he had more important people who required his attention.

Carter stepped closer to the headmaster, looking him squarely in the eyes to let him know that he had no intention of allowing Mr. Wirth to walk off without Carter's having made his point. Mr. Wirth looked away nervously, then looked back at Carter acquiescently.

"Not long ago," Carter began," I sat in your office while you referred to that student you just congratulated as a fudge packer. Anyway, now that he's leaving, has gotten into Princeton, is about to set the world on fire, I suppose you've decided to overlook that incident, pretend that it never happened."

"Again, Mr. Moran, what is this about? I have people to greet," Mr. Wirth replied, small beads of sweat collecting on his brow.

"Look, after today, I'm leaving here, and whether I come back here, whether I'm invited back, is probably irrelevant to you. But if I don't get a written apology from you, a detailed written apology—"

"What?" Mr. Wirth interrupted impatiently, stepping back and looking around to see if anyone had taken notice of the brief contretemps taking place between him and the new young faculty member.

"I'll go to my contact at the *Post* and tell them how, behind closed doors, the headmaster of the Melbourne School refers to its students as fudge packers," Carter warned with a tremble in his voice.

"And you think that will somehow tarnish the reputation of this school?" Mr. Wirth retorted indignantly, as if to take the dare.

"I know it will. Because for all of its conservative values, this is still an institution of learning, and learned people don't belittle their best and brightest by referring to them as fudge packers," Carter scolded, his face red, seething with anger.

"And you think people will pay attention to you?"

"They will when I bring our little discussion to the attention of Mr. and Mrs. Jack Fitz-Waring," Carter paused, regaining his composure. "You know, the ones on Melbourne's board of directors. You probably don't know that Mrs. Fitz-Waring is a published author, a good one," Carter continued.

Mr. Wirth smirked as if he found little point in what Carter was saying. "And?" he said.

"She wrote a book a few years ago about what it felt like when her son came out as a homosexual," Carter continued, reveling in the shock he could see on Mr. Wirth's face.

"Not the son who went here, you'll be relieved to know," Carter continued, "but the older boy. The book wasn't a best-seller, so you probably never read it or even knew about it. But I think the Fitz-Warings would find your comments very disagreeable. And I know other people will pay attention to them, even if they don't pay attention to me," Carter finished with a smile, gloating in vindication.

"That's absurd! This is extortion!" Mr. Wirth exclaimed defensively.

"Call it whatever you want. But I'll expect that apology—that detailed apology—within ten days. I've left my forwarding address with Mrs. Brockman. She'll know where to send it."

"This is preposterous."

"Call it whatever you like. But I want an apology."

Mr. Wirth paused, looking down at the ground disgustedly, then glanced away from Carter and said, "You'll get it. Now excuse me." And with that, he skulked away.

Carter was not sure why he had demanded what he did. He knew he would not change Mr. Wirth's attitude, but somehow he hoped that in the future, Mr. Wirth would not take such a hostile, cavalier attitude toward students like Adam Proffit—toward students who were, in his own words, "different." Carter hoped that somehow the Melbourne School would become a better place for it. But most of all, he wanted to leave Melbourne with some sense of having vindicated Adam and all of the other students like him, who had been there before or who would inevitably attend there after. Carter smiled briefly, then walked back to his apartment to gather the remainder of his things.

When Carter reached the top of the stairs, he walked past his apartment and down the long hall of the dormitory, opened one of the windows, and stepped out onto the roof. He climbed up to the top of the roof, slipping a few times on the old slate tiles, until he reached the summit of the Monroe Building. There, he sat down and took in the vast expanse of the Blue Ridge Mountains, misted green in springtime foliage. He could see the crowds of students gathered with their parents, friends, and other family. Adam was likely still down there somewhere, which caused Carter to smile. *You're gonna make it, Adam Proffit. You've made it this far, and I look forward to seeing where you go next.*

THE END

978-0-595-37435-9
0-595-37435-2

Lightning Source UK Ltd.
Milton Keynes UK
23 October 2009

145301UK00002B/140/A